DATE DUE

M
M.

Donovan's Station

Other books by Robin McGrath
available through Creative Book Publishing

POETRY
Escaped Domestics (1998)
ISBN 0-920021-57-3
$12.95

SHORT STORIES
Trouble and Desire (1996)
ISBN 0-920021-36-0
$11.95

YOUNG ADULT
Hoist Your Sails and Run (1999)
ISBN 0-920021-78-6
$11.95

Ask your favourite bookstore or order directly from the publisher.

Creative Book Publishing
P.O. Box 8660
36 Austin Street
St. John's, NF
A1B 3T7

phone: (709) 722-8500
fax: (709) 579-7745
e-mail: books@rb.nf.ca
URL: www.nfbooks.com

Please add $5.00 Canadian for shipping and handling and taxes on single book orders and $1.00 for each additional book.

Donovan's Station

a novel

ROBIN MCGRATH

St. John's, Newfoundland
2002

Le Conseil des Arts | The Canada Council
du Canada | for the Arts

We acknowledge the support of The Canada Council for the Arts for our publishing
program.

We acknowledge the financial support of the Government of Canada through the Book
Publishing Industry Development Program (BPIDP) for our publishing
program.

Front Cover Art: Photo of Betsy Donovan
Back Cover Art: Photo of Donovan's Station
All photos from McGrath family collection
Cover Design: John Andrews

∞ Printed on acid-free paper

Published by
KILLICK PRESS
an imprint of CREATIVE BOOK PUBLISHING
a Trancontinental associated company
P.O. Box 8660, St. John's, Newfoundland and Labrador
A1B 3T7

Second Printing February 2004
Typeset in 12.5 point Centaur

Printed in Canada by:
TRANSCONTINENTAL

National Library of Canada Cataloguing in Publication Data

McGrath, Robin
    Donovan's station: a novel / Robin McGrath.

ISBN 1-894294-42-4

    1. Newfoundland and Labrador--Fiction. I. Title.

PS8575.G73D65 2002   C813'.54   C2002-901661-4
PR9199.3.M42427D65 2002

For Janet Kelly

May 22, 1914

Archbishop Howley,
The Palace
St. John's

Your Grace,
Enclosed are the papers you requested for your trip to Europe. I have been in touch with Brother Power in Tralee and have arranged for him to be with you throughout your stay in Ireland. I only wish I had as much confidence in the assistance I have organized for your sojourns in Spain and Italy, and that you will not be too greatly fatigued by the journey and the labours that accompany it.

During your absence, I intend to plan out the structural reorganization of the administration that you have approved, and see only one major impediment to be overcome. Merging the various convents under a single mother house would benefit the Catholic education system immensely, but unfortunately the nuns appear to be firmly wedded to the system as it was designed by the late Bishop Fleming. While it may be possible to order compliance, it would be better achieved through negotiation.

As you are no doubt aware, I have in my Topsail parish an acquaintance of the Bishop, one Keziah Donovan, the proprietress of the flag stop station at St. Ann's. She has old ties with the Presentation Sisters and if she could be persuaded to give her support to the scheme it might be all that is needed to make it happen. I am assuming, of course, that the Bishop was scrupulous in his dealings with the woman. Evidence to the contrary might lessen the hold his memory has on the members of the order.

Mrs. Donovan is very elderly, and I had news this morning that she may be in failing health. Discreet inquiry indicates that any documents relevant to our concerns such as wills, letters etc., are in the hands of the Railway's lawyer. Conroy is one of our own staunchest supporters, a friend of the Church, and would warn you if there were any compromising correspondence in his hands. My intention is not to discredit the parties involved, but to protect the good reputation of one of the most respected members of our community. A reminder that you answer directly to Rome might be in order.

Your intercession with His Holiness, and the proposal of my name for elevation to the position of Domestic Prelate at the Papal Throne, is an honour that I can only say was beyond my greatest imagining. I can assure you that the affairs of the Archdiocese of St. John's may be safely trusted to me as Administrator during your absence, and after your return for as long as I am needed.

> Your most obliged and very
> obedient humble servant
> Edward Patrick Roche, Vicar-General

May 23

Very fine, cool day. Doctor has been, and says that Mumma has had a paralytic stroke. Dermot forgot the bacon for the Society dinner; will have to make-do with fat-back. Kaiser William wandered onto the track and they had to stop the train. It took three men to push him off and one got kicked. Had a note from Monsignor Roche asking after Mumma. So kind of him—I didn't think they got along but he sounded quite concerned.

The crows are racketing—the train must be on its way. Funny how the crows always make such a fuss about the train, as if it were an owl or an animal that has to be scared off. It works, of course. They give the Irish cry as the train pulls towards the station, and the thing goes off again, leaving the cows and the farm to them.

The eleven fifteen was late as usual, no doubt. I hope they sent out the bacon to wrap the partridges for the dinner tonight. Or was that last night? No use fussing—I can't do anything about it anyway and it only wears at me. The Benevolent Irishmen, or the Orangemen, or the Mechanics' Society, or whoever it was wanted partridges will no doubt survive without me to feed them. Kate will always manage somehow.

Now the train is going, the 107. I can always tell that engine, it has such a huffy sound to it, like young Lizzie when she isn't getting her own way. Is Lizzie here or in town? I can't remember what day it is. It seems so odd to be lying down in broad daylight, staring at the ceiling, with all that work in the kitchen to be done. Peaceful, though, with the crows and the train, and the sound of Kate's cows in back. Kate wanted to move me into her room, away from the train and the traffic, but I like the sound of the world going by my door; it's soothing, really, and it distracts me from worrying about whether someone will stop and want something we don't have.

I know I can't move, but it doesn't feel like it. I thought paralysis would feel like you were frozen and no matter how hard you tried you couldn't budge, but for once in my life I have no desire to move at all. If I could lift my hand this instant I wouldn't do it, not unless my sweet man was to hold his hand out to me and urge me to take his in mine, and that won't happen as he's seven years in the graveyard. "Happy as a lamb on a tombstone," he used to say when I asked him if there was anything he wanted at the end of a meal. And at the last going off he said, "No lambs, maidey, not 'til you're there with me." So the marble lamb sits in the back shed, packed in straw, waiting for me to go too, and I suppose that won't be long now. Not if I can learn to keep my mouth shut when Lizzie's around.

Eighty-four years is time enough for one life. My dear Mr. Donovan was only sixty-seven when he died. Too young. Ah, I can feel the water leaking out of my eyes at the very thought of him. Mustn't do that, for if Kate looks in she'll worry. Kate has enough to worry about, with the dinners for the Benevolent Irishmen and young Lizzie nagging her about how she dresses, and now me stuck here like a bump on a log, dying too slowly.

If only my mouth were paralyzed. I try not to eat, but they coax me and eventually I give in and have a mouthful and before I know it that's turned to three or four mouthfuls. How long has it been now? A week, perhaps. There is just too much of me to disappear in a single week. I know I'm losing weight, for when Kate turns me over now I can tell it's easier for her, and when I look down I have to try harder to see the swell of the bed cover.

Last night—I think it was last night—they sent Lizzie with the apple and I could smell it as she came into the room. My heart sank down through the mattress, for I knew I couldn't say no to an apple. Kate had stuffed it with Demerara sugar and butter, and baked it to mush with a little grating of nutmeg, just the way I used to do it for her and Min and Johanna when they were little and had a cough or a sore throat. Lizzie sat so that I could see her face—so like mine when I was fourteen—and she said "You're going to eat, Nanny," and I thought how like her it was to be bossing me around even when I'm on my deathbed.

That face of hers—it's so peculiar to see her eyes looking out of my face. We're as different as chalk and cheese, me and Lizzie. I was always soft, easy to shift, and Lizzie is like steel. If she ever falls in love, it will be a terrible shock to her. She sat there with the spoon and the apple and told me to open my mouth and when I didn't she leaned over and kissed me, right on my lips, and I was so astonished that I opened up. Before I knew it she had half the apple spooned down my throat, and I almost laughed to see the triumph in her eyes. She'll be berating poor Kate that it's her fault I'm not eating. I hope Min comes and takes her home again soon, so we can all get some rest.

I must keep my teeth together next time.

> *Thirty white horses upon a red hill;*
> *Now they stamp, now they champ, now they*
> *stand still.*

I haven't got thirty white horses left—only twenty three last time I counted—and they were never really white, but they have lasted me eighty-four years so I suppose I mustn't complain against them now. I used to hate my teeth, clamped my mouth shut even when I smiled so that no one would have to look at those square, yellow pickets, but they were strong and when other women my age were losing their teeth, mine just went on champing and stamping. Old habits die hard, though, and only sweet Mr. Donovan could make me smile outright. It was just shyness gave me a mouth like an axe—in Lizzie, it's grit. I see the determination in the set of her mouth and I don't wonder any more that people didn't know I am just shy.

The shadows are different; I must have fallen asleep. And here comes another train, a special excursion going out to Kelligrews, perhaps. I remember the first time I saw the train, in January of '82 it was, just the two cars and half a dozen men hanging off the engine. They stopped over at Ann Fitzpatrick's and the engineer had burned his waistcoat and it reminded me of the Bishop. How Bishop Fleming would have loved the train. He was such a man for traveling, always off to Europe to raise money for the convents or to build the Cathedral or to fight with the Anglicans over the twelve shilling fee for Catholic burials, and when he was home it was off up the coast to Fogo or wherever. He'd never have let the train go by, day after day for thirty-two years, and not gotten on it to see what was at the end of the line.

I used to wonder about the places it went, what meals the other station hotels and inns were serving to the passengers, but somehow there always seemed so much to do here that getting on the train when it was outward bound just didn't happen. Lizzie can't believe that I've never been west of Kelligrews. I've been south to Petty Harbour, east as far as the Battery, and north to Broad Cove, and I know every inch of the land between. I've walked it, rode it on horseback, driven it in carriages and long carts, even done most of it one time or another in Mr. Goodridge's motor car. I know every stick and stone from Paradise and the Horse Cove Line to Fort William. In my younger days, I could find my way in the thickest fog or a driving snowstorm as easily as if it was a sunny day in September. Even the Bishop didn't know the route as well as I did.

Now here's a thought. I will see the Bishop soon if I can just shut my teeth against the baked apples. That's who I'll look for, as soon as ever I've found my own sweet man, Mr. Donovan. I'm sure Bishop Fleming will like Mr. Donovan. I must tell him about the train, though perhaps people in heaven already know everything there is to know. Still, I'll tell him about the engineer and the waistcoat, as it will make him laugh. Perhaps in heaven I will remember the burnt waistcoat but not Mrs. Cadigan's baby.

Oh, I can feel the water on my face again. I am so weak. I can't shut my mouth against the sweet apples and I can't shut my eyes against the salt tears. So long ago. I can't remember a thing before that day, not even my baby brother being born. The Bishop was at the stove stirring the pot and he fell asleep and burned his waistcoat. I will think about the work, carrying the food to the houses, and it will dry the tears. Five, I must have been, and sturdy even then, and so lucky not to have caught the smallpox when everyone else was sick and dying with it. My father got it first, spots like bird shot under the skin of his wrists, and then just as he was getting a little better Mother got sick and then Richard got it, and neither of them able to lift a finger to do anything for the poor little boy. I did what I could, keeping the fire going in the stove and soaking out a bit of fish and biscuit to feed us all, but I was only five and I'd been waited on hand and foot my whole short life. That changed soon enough.

I was looking out the window, I don't know why because everyone in Petty Harbour was either gone or sick, and that's when I saw the Bishop coming over the hill. He had his skirts hiked up into his belt and he had a bag on his back with his medical chest in it. I remember, I ran and told my mother there was a black man coming, meaning a clergyman, and when she looked and saw it was a Catholic priest she started to cry, thinking she'd get no help from him. Maybe if it had been another man, she'd have been right, but Bishop Fleming never asked who was Catholic and who wasn't, he just set to, trying to help feed everyone.

I think we were the only house on the Southside with a stove then. Everyone else had an open fireplace, with crooks and crottles for hanging the pots on, or iron fire dogs and a crane if they were lucky, and I thought it was such a pity to shut the fire up in a box but my mother was so proud of that stove. Grandfather Bulley had sent it out when Richard was born, a gift for his first grandson.

There now, I do remember before the Bishop. I was so small, I hadn't realized how much trouble it was to keep an open fire, or how hard it was to cook on one. Father had cut enough wood for the whole winter when the smallpox came, so the Bishop used our house for cooking the food, what there was of it. "The Bishop's little rodney" they called me, because I followed him around the Harbour the whole winter, carrying pots of food across to the Catholics on the Northside as well as to the Protestants on the South. I still have the scar on my ankle where I spilled hot water down my boot. I was such a baby— people were dying all around me and I was crying my eyes out over a blister the size of a penny, but the Bishop put chamomile salve on it and wrapped it in scorched cloth just as if it was a real injury.

I can almost smell the bandage now, the hot, clean smell of the burnt linen so different from the scorched smell of his waistcoat. He was so tired, he must have fallen asleep standing up at the stove and I smelled the wool of his vest burning. "Bishop, dearest," I said, pulling on his coat tails, for I was such a baby I didn't know you mustn't call a bishop 'dearest'. "Bishop, dearest, wake up or you will burn the dinner," I said, and he staggered back from the pot and almost lost his balance, and his waistcoat was steaming. He was making a sort of porridge, using whatever he could find, oatmeal and flour and hard biscuit all boiled up in water, and then he'd put a lashing of molasses into it from the keg in the corner, and we'd carry it around the Harbour, to the houses where the people were too sick to cook anything.

It was the day he burned his waistcoat that we went out to see the Cadigans. Theirs was the last house on the path out to town, and they'd all been fine when the Bishop came into the Harbour, so he hadn't worried about them, thinking, I suppose, that they were too far away to be infected. But then he noticed that there was no smoke coming from there two days in a row, so we went round with the food and saved a bit in case they needed it. They were all dead except the baby. Mr. Cadigan was wrapped up in a blanket on the floor by the wall, and the older boy was on a mat near the fireplace, and Mrs. Cadigan was in the bed, covered in sores from the pox. The baby was covered in sores as well, but it was still alive and the smell of the place was enough to choke you. Poor little baby, so sad, only it had managed to get the clothes off its mother and had gnawed at her breasts 'til she was half eaten.

The Bishop must have forgotten I was there, for he took the Lord's name in vain, though I'm sure the Lord will have forgiven him considering the circumstances. I must have made a noise, dropped the little bucket I was carrying, perhaps, because he turned around and flung his arms round my head, pulling me tight to his waist so I wouldn't see, and I could smell the burnt wool of his waistcoat, such a relief after the smell in the room where the baby had done its business all over the bed, and the poor little thing died before we got halfway home with it. We buried it in an empty nail keg. I remember thinking it might have been my baby brother, and I never wanted to mind Richard after that.

I suppose if I could lift my hands, I could say a rosary for the Bishop's soul, but he probably doesn't need rosaries. I'd have offered up a lifetime of rosaries for him already, if I'd thought for a moment that he really needed them. October 7th, he came, which is the feast of Our Lady of the Holy Rosary, he told me later. I was too small to know at the time and besides we were all Anglicans then. The feast was to celebrate the defeat of the Turks at the battle of Lepanto, wherever that is. Maybe it's in Carpasia—after all, he was Bishop of Carpasia, not really Bishop of Newfoundland.

It was Bishop Fleming who taught me to say the rosary, and I have said it thousands and thousands of times since—the Joyful Mysteries for my father, who learned to be content with having just a daughter, the Sorrowful Mysteries for my mother who lost the only child she really loved, although she did her best to hide that from me, and the Glorious Mysteries which I said first for nobody in particular but that I now know were really for Mr. Donovan.

The Bishop taught me my letters too. I'm sure he wanted me to be a school teacher, but he showed me too clearly the blessing of feeding people during his winter in Petty Harbour. A was an apple pie, and everything that follows does so because apple pie is good to eat. "C cut it", he'd say, and using a bit of charred stick he's draw the letter C on the side of the pail full of porridge, so I'd know I was to bring it to the Clearys on the Northside. L longed for it—that went to the Lees, on the Southside. M mourned for it. Morris, Southside. He drew me out the whole alphabet on oilcloth, and sewed it into a tiny book: "The Tragical Death of A, Apple Pie, Who was Cut in Pieces and Eaten by Twenty-six Gentlemen, With Whom all Little People Ought to be Very Well Acquainted".

By Christmas, I knew all the letters, even the ones like X and Z that had no names, so he began to teach me words other than names. There were no books, except his breviary and our

Bible, so he taught me to read from the Bible and it is a habit I have retained all my life, though it is not a very Roman thing to do. "What do you want with that?" asked Paddy, when I put the Bible in with the linen to move to town with him after we were married. "They've got one in the church. The priest will read it to us if we need to know it." Not that he went to church much. He'd make a show of going, stand in the back with the other men for a while, and then drift off out the door, to smoke his pipe and talk, or away to O'Neil's for a drink of rum.

Poor Paddy. Perhaps if I had loved him more he would have come to church with me, but he loved himself such a great deal that there wasn't really room for anyone else to love him. Certainly our girls loved him, but he saw them as part of himself, like his hands or feet. I'm glad they were grown and gone, except Kate, of course, when I married Mr. Donovan. They couldn't approve of anyone taking their father's place. I could never bring myself to call Mr. Donovan by his first name, it being the same as Paddy's, and I know they thought it was a delicacy in me, an unwillingness to use the holy name of Paddy Aylward on a man they thought was his inferior, but the truth is that it was the other way around. I loved my darling Mr. Donovan so much that I couldn't bear to call him by a name that was ashes in my mouth.

Did the Bishop know what he was doing when he married me off to Paddy Aylward? The Bishop was such a good man, and he had such faith in me, that he may have thought I would save Paddy's soul and so he offered me up as a sacrifice. I'm afraid I let him down. It wasn't such a bad marriage, I suppose. Paddy was sober when he had to be, and he never laid a finger on me in anger except the once. We raised three fine girls, and buried only one beautiful baby. He was a hard worker in life and he left me provided for after he died. Can anyone ask for more? Oh, yes, for there is more, and I got it eventually.

I must ask Kate about the bacon. The partridges will be too

dry without it. I tried to remind her yesterday, but she didn't seem to be able to understand me. My head is so clear, now, that I'm sure I will be able to talk. I must remember, though, not to try to speak if she has a spoon in her hand or she will be sure to put food in my mouth. The sooner I learn to keep my mouth shut when there is a spoon, the sooner I will be with my sweet Mr. Donovan and my dearest Bishop.

Now they stamp, now they champ, now they stand still.

May 28

Fine day. Attended mass at Topsail while Mrs. Walsh stayed with Mumma. Home in time to do the teas. Had to redo the pastry—the girl forgot to add vinegar to the cold water and it was dunchy. The place will go to ruin without Mumma. Her eyes never stop searching the ceiling. What is she looking for? Had a most unnerving visit from Monsignor Roche, who said he'd wanted to speak to me after mass. How was I to know? I know I am not an imposing figure like Mumma, but he makes me feel so small and insignificant that I want to crawl into the milk house and hide. When he calls, I wish we had just an ordinary parish priest, the kind who likes a short rosary and second helpings. We have the Newsboys on Wednesday. Last year they rode on the cows and almost drowned two hens in the river. Please God, Dermot will lend a hand.

Father Roche was here and left without even a glass of port, for I heard the door slam behind him and I know Kate wouldn't have forgotten to offer something. I am uneasy with a priest who doesn't drink at least a little. He spoke to Kate as if she were deaf, asking about whether the doctor thought I'd recover and then quizzing her on how much I talked to her about the old days and my friendship with Bishop Fleming. He said if I recovered, he'd like to talk to me about it. Nothing would give me greater pleasure than to remind Father Roche of the stirling qualities of the man who first held the office he aspires to.

Dear Bishop Fleming was such a blessing to the poor people here—so anxious for the fishermen and their families who had little or nothing. They came with nothing and after all their labours, they often had nothing but more mouths to feed at the end of a season. And the poor babies—not a cuff or a vamp, and sometimes not even a shirt to cover their poor bare bottoms. But such compassion the Bishop had, even for the improvident. Father Roche will need a bigger heart than those usually found in Placentia Bay men if he is to fill the Bishop's shoes.

My parents were more fortunate than most in the way they settled here, although some would say there is no such thing as good fortune unless you make it yourself. That is what my mother always said, and it is what I told Judge Prowse when he asked me to tell him of the circumstances surrounding my people's settling here. I suppose it was really an accident of the weather. They came out heading for Upper Canada, but their ship ran into difficulty and took refuge in St. John's Harbour, short of food, full of water, and half sinking. Mother had friends in the Garrison—coney kin, I believe—and insisted on disembarking while the ship was refitted, and during the stopover they decided to stay on and go over to Grates Cove where there were some distant relatives of Father. The cod fishery was looking pretty grim at the time, but sealing was a growing industry and during their stay the whelping ice came in, jamming between the point and Baccalieu Island, and my parents were instantly transformed into landsmen for the course of one week. The judge rubbed his hands in satisfaction when I told him that, and pencilled a little note in the book he always carried in his pocket.

Father always teased Mother about that occasion, brief as it was, and said that if he ever gave up fishing he'd arrange to send her to the ice on one of the sealing vessels to support the family. Mother rarely did more than pull a face at this remark, but I could tell there was a mixture of pride and regret in her at the memory. Having been raised on a farm, she had more than a passing familiarity with the bloodier elements, and had learned as a young child to castrate pigs and kill chickens—her father had some form of palsy and considered her hand steadier than his own—and it was with her encouragement that Father went out on the ice that spring day at Grates Cove. Father was a great fish killer but he had never before killed a fur-bearing animal, and the sound of the whitecoats bawling—as like a human infant as one can imagine—unnerved him dreadfully. After he had taken the first few pelts and towed them back to shore, Mother's frustration at watching him do things in such a tentative and clumsy way led her to shed her coat and tuck her skirts up to show him how to dispatch an animal properly.

It is hard, now, to imagine my mother, so small and contained in her person, taking on the butchery of sealing, but I suppose she saw shillings in the eyes of every seal on the ice and determined not to let them escape her hands if she could do anything about it. Father said she was wearing a bright red jacket that was stained with oil and blood within moments, but she told him he could buy her a dozen jackets with the money they would make at the sealing. She did the butchering and flensing and he towed the pelts back to shore, collecting not just hers but others that were left panned on the ice. The seals were so numerous that people simply killed them and piled the pelts up indiscriminately as the week went on, leaving them for whoever had the rope and the energy to tow them ashore. She was not the only woman to turn her hand to the seals—whole families were out, with kettles left cold on the stoves and babies left crying in their cribs.

Father said that as the week wore on, he became more and more worried that the wind would turn and take them all out to sea, and he became reluctant to let Mother out of his sight. Once he turned to look back and could not see her and thought she had gone through a rent in the ice, but she was only hidden behind a hummock. Another time he lost sight of her for only a moment and he was so exhausted that, in tracking back towards her, he followed a man in a red flannel shirt for two miles before realizing his error. Finally, he could take no more and insisted that they stop and be satisfied with what they had. That night, three women and a boy were lost and never seen again when the ice moved off unexpectedly.

Father was all for settling in Grates Cove after that, but Mother was only seventeen and the place had little appeal for her, so after a time they went to have another look at St. John's again. I believe it was her intention to open a small shop, making clothes and hats, but Father was still attached to the fishery, and besides he found the stench and noise of St. John's disturbing to his constitution, so after a winter in town they moved on to Petty Harbour where he used the cash from the sealing bonanza to build a skiff and set up rooms. There was no road to town then, but there was an Indian path and since it was only ten miles from St. John's it was not as isolated as Grates Cove. At Mother's urging, they purchased a small cutover lot from a tilter who was moving on—at that time there were few land grants and no formal titles, just occupation, but the tilters had their own system for ascertaining ownership of land—and it was here they established Mother's gardens.

I think that my father never quite got used to the availability of wood in such quantities as we had near Petty Harbour. There were times when I saw him stop and gaze at a stand of spruce or fir and he would laugh aloud at the absurdity of being able to go and cut as much of it as he wanted without paying anyone a penny for the privilege. Men who had settled only a few years before he did complained bitterly that the woods around the harbour were chopped and burned to nothing, and if they couldn't reach out their hand and cut a stick to put on the fire without getting out of their beds they were aggrieved, but for Father to travel five, ten, even twenty miles to find knees for his boats was nothing, and he often hauled our winter wood from fairly long distances.

Whatever he could make, he did, and insisted Mother do the same. Despite the promise of a dozen red jackets, I never knew her to wear anything but homespun although she always had a way of making even the coarsest clothing look delicate. Coin was so rare in those days that few could afford to purchase imported furniture or clothing, but most people got at least a few things from home. Such wasn't the case with us. The table and two chairs we had—for we children used three-legged stools—were carved by my father during the long winter days when he would set a block of snow outside the small window near the stove to reflect light in so that he and Mother could work. He had no tools for turning legs but he carved them so perfectly that only the most discerning eye could tell the difference. My mother spun wool whenever she wasn't busy with anything else—could do it in her sleep, she said.

I believe the only things we had that were imported were a few dishes, the stove from Grandfather Bulley and our Argand lamp, and that last was used only on relatively rare occasions as Father was concerned that the oil would corrode the mechanism and leave us with no proper light in an emergency. Like most of the people in the Harbour, we rose with the sun, and went to bed with it as well. During winter, when the days were short, Mother and Father would often sit by the stove for a time late in the evening, using the dim light from the mica insert in the front of the stove to finish some small job, and Richard and I would listen to the quiet murmuring of their voices until we fell asleep or they climbed the loft to join us in bed. I occasionally heard them disagree—Mother wanting to raise more goats or plant more turnips than Father thought we could use, or Father wishing to hire on as a servant someone Mother felt was giddy or unreliable—but I never heard them raise their voices in anger, nor did I ever hear my mother weep for her lost hat-shop or her red jacket.

June 2

Fine, cool day. No change in Mumma. Wish Lizzie would visit.

There's a bluebottle at the window that keeps me restless. I hope Kate comes soon to deal with it. I have such a nervous mind today, and for once I am glad I can't speak for almost anything could come out of my mouth and there are some things best forgotten. I'm glad I settled the matter of the grave when Mr. Donovan died, for that's one worry off my mind. I'd have preferred to be buried in town, but we belong to Topsail parish and he liked the view out over the bay, so I chose a nice double plot well back from the gate so we would be away from the tramp and curiosity of casual passersby. We always liked our own company best. Pity we never had our own grave-yard here at St. Ann's, but I suppose with no church, and the hotel, it wasn't really practical.

That was a nice graveyard in Petty Harbour that the Bishop set up after the smallpox epidemic. Perhaps that is what Father Roche wishes to talk about. There was some problem at the time that I did not understand—a petition had gone from several of the Protestant families to Governor Prescott with the professed object of preventing the removal of the interred remains of some of their deceased friends from the chapel-yard to the new cemetery, but common sense prevailed. When the Bishop had first arrived the previous fall, there had been three deaths from the pox and the graveyard, which was in the middle of the town, was already a considerable threat to the health of the inhabitants. Some of the graves were within three and four yards of the doors of the houses, virtually on top of some of the wells, and it was necessary to make a more hygienic arrangement.

One of the first things the Bishop did, once he was settled with his medicine chest in a small waste house near the church, was to locate a piece of land half a mile distant where there was sufficient soil to cover the bodies of the dead. Those most recently interred were quickly removed to this more suitable place, a process I recall watching with a somewhat morbid fascination, and then of course the Cadigan baby and his family quickly joined them. As the temperature continued to drop and the critically ill grew less threatened, the Bishop convinced the men to move as many more of the graves as they could identify. He then, at his own expense, purchased a piece of ground adjoining the old cemetery and, by blasting the rocks, reduced it to a level that allowed him to begin the construction of our fine little church. The dear man had the heart of a cleric but the eye and ambition of an architect.

The Protestant petition was motivated, I suppose, by sectarianism from the outside, for the Bishop was on terms of the best friendship with ourselves and all our Protestant neighbours, and the suggestion that he was interrupting the repose of the mortal remains of our relatives was nonsense. Most of us did not have close relatives in the Harbour, having emigrated to the colony only relatively recently. The majority of the graves in the community, some of which were scattered between and even under the houses—in any small ditch or hollow that afforded cover—were those of transient fishermen who had come out as servants or dieters. Unbaptized babies, of which there were a surprising number, were disposed of almost anywhere. In later years, on at least two occasions, I unearthed bones in my garden that I am quite certain belonged to humans.

The little square of level ground that the Bishop had cut into the rock stood empty for several months through the winter while he waited for Governor Prescott to intervene with the Anglican clergy on his behalf, and as most work was stopped by illness and bad weather it afforded us children a fine new place for playing. There were hardly six square yards of flat ground in the entire district, so it was a great novelty for us to have somewhere we could run and gatch without fear of tumbling down a hillside or into the sea. Some of the boys played a game called tiddly, employing any sticks and stones they could find about the place—the rules of this game were and still are a mystery to me—but mostly we just used the space for running about.

When the Catholics finally got a church, of course the Protestants had to have a new church too, but that made no odds to us. I preferred St. David's to St. Andrew's, perhaps because I knew the old church but never set foot in the new one. Our own had the superior bell, for St. Andrew's bell came out of an old ship while ours was a gift of the Bishop of Hamburg, and it produced a fine, pretty sound that must have rung in the ears of Napoleon himself in his day. They say it came out of a pre-Reformation monastery.

There was little division between the Catholics and the Protestants in Petty Harbour, other than a geographic one which was the result of when each group arrived rather than deliberate separation, but there was an awareness that the two groups were on two sides of a fence that was troublesome to cross over. It was a fence that the Bishop worked to remove and that Father Roche would build up again. I myself was made painfully aware of this barrier as I grew older, because of my special relationship with the Bishop.

There was current, at that time, a children's rhyme or game that was often played out for my benefit. A boy, or more often a girl, would pull her hands up into the sleeves of her coat and stick a knuckle out of each cuff, affecting a gruff or falsetto voice. The following dialogue would ensue:

> *Good Morning, Father Francis.*
> *Good Morning, Mrs. Murphy, what takes you abroad so early?*
> *Oh, Father Francis, I have committed a great sin and have to go to confession.*
> *And what is that great sin, Mrs. Murphy?*
> *Your cat stole a fish off my flake, Father Francis.*
> *Sure, 'tis no sin at all, Mrs. Murphy.*
> *But I killed your cat, Father.*
> *Then 'tis a very grave sin, Mrs. Murphy; you will have to do penance.*
> *And what would that penance be?*
> *You must kiss me three times.*
> *Oh, but I can't.*
> *Oh, but you must.*
> *Well, if I must, I must.*
> *Kiss, kiss, kiss, and away.*

At the last line, the hands would pop out of the sleeves and there would be general laughter all round with a sly look in my direction.

I believe that the nuns were responsible for making more of my friendship with the Bishop than was warranted by his small attention to me. It is true that when I was five, I did not hesitate to climb into his lap and demand a kiss in exchange for any small errand. I quickly learned to keep myself to myself and by the time I was in school I never put myself forward during his annual visit but waited for him to ask for me. I doubt I saw him more than once every year or eighteen months, and never heard from him directly although he very occasionally sent a brief message through my mother expressing his affection and his hopes for my future. He treated me like a niece or young cousin that he took an interest in but knew little of. It was the nuns who behaved as if this was some extraordinary blessing that had been bestowed on me and that I had best exert myself.

It is true that my association with the Bishop, tenuous as it was, made me feel special in some way. My own father was a fond and indulgent parent, but he had such a dire outlook on life that when I was around him I found it necessary to suppress my natural instinct for happiness. I believe my mother must have laboured under the same oppression, but she was more outgoing by nature than I and better able to struggle against his melancholy. The Bishop was the opposite—always building, planning, raising money for the churches and schools and convents that now stand as monuments to his energy and optimism. If on the outside I emulated my father's guarded solemnity and sobriety, inside I could feel the Bishop's hope and gaiety surging upward. The Bishop once said I was his spiritual child, and in this he was right, for no matter how difficult things got, I never lost my belief that I could improve my lot through hard work and effort.

The summer after the epidemic, the church was consecrated, all the impediments having been removed through the kind intervention of Governor Prescott and the churchyard having been completed. On the 15th of May, Bishop Fleming confirmed over 400 people in the church at Petty Harbour, close to fifty of these being converts who had decided to join the Catholic Church out of gratitude for his having looked after the Anglicans on the Southside as tenderly as he cared for the Catholics on the Northside when the smallpox ravaged our little town.

My mother, Richard and I were among those confirmed, and I know it was the source of some pain to my mother that

Father did not join us in this enterprise. I remember clearly that we all dressed for the occasion and he came to the church with us, but when I knelt before the Bishop and received his slight blow on my cheek, my mother was there but my father was not. Father attended mass with us whenever there was a priest available, and at night when we said our evening prayers he knelt with us, but he never took the sacraments nor did he ever discuss the matter in our presence. This was something between my parents that was as private and hidden as those other secret aspects of married life that I came to know only as an adult.

After Richard drowned, my mother never regained her enthusiasm for life and turned more and more inward, away from my father and me and towards the church, the priest, and the life to come. The transition took several years, and time and again, particularly during the long winter evenings that had been such a source of companionship and comfort to them in the past, I saw my father look at her with such a longing and sadness that I feared for him as well as for her. When it was clear that she was dying, Father sent for Bishop Fleming who came to us immediately. It had been the Bishop's usual practice, and that of all the priests who visited the Harbour before and since, to stay at Mr. Kielly's, the only exception being the winter of the epidemic when he feared infecting those good people, but on this occasion he directed me to make up a bed on a low trestle in the kitchen, and it was here he slept after administering extreme unction to my mother.

During the night, my mother went to her final reward, happy in the knowledge that she was joining her darling boy, and saddened only by the awareness that her husband had not yet realized his error and joined the true church. Her last petition to me was that I pray unceasingly for his soul, and I would have done so had it not been for the events which followed. Because the Bishop was wanted back in St. John's, the funeral was held immediately. Bishop Fleming conducted the mass, led the men to the graveyard and with my father saw the body placed in the earth beside Richard, and returned to the house to take a small collation before leaving to walk back over the hills to town.

Throughout all of this my father was quiet and attentive, ensuring that the Bishop ate and drank as well as possible, thanking him on my behalf and his own for such kind attention, and before he left handing over a substantial sum of the Spanish and English coins our family had so painstakingly accumulated as a donation to the new Cathedral of St. John the Baptist, the foundations of which had just been laid. As soon as the Bishop was out of sight, my father stripped the bedding from the trestle he had slept on and pulled it into the path outside the house. There it was soon joined by the chair the Bishop had sat on, the dishes he had eaten from, the very table at which he had taken his meal, every object he had touched. Father burnt them all to ashes so that no taint of papism was left in his house, with the not-inconsiderable exception of myself.

This mad and uncharacteristic expression of my father's grief must have been reported to the Bishop, for some days later I received a brief visit from Father Edward Troy, the Bishop's former vicar-general. My father was back at his fishing, and I was uncomfortable about receiving the priest into the house behind his back, but he made no attempt to pass through the door. I was grateful for this, for what in the Bishop was zeal and enthusiasm, in Father Troy bordered on obsession and fanaticism. He told me that my friend had asked him to convey his personal conviction that my father's generosity to the church, and his tolerance of my own adherence to the true faith, would surely open the gates of heaven when the time was right, and I was not to worry myself about the matter. It was clear that the message Father Troy brought was one he did not agree with, which only served to reassure me that the Bishop knew best, and from that moment on I left the care of my father's soul in the

capable hands of one who was much closer to our Heavenly
Father than I was.

June 6

Thick fog and cold. One of the cows has as ulcer. Must not mention it to Mumma as I know who she will blame. I am so used to telling her all the small details of the household business that I feel bottled up and ready to overflow with talk, but it makes her fret.

I can hear the cows lowing. Where is that Big Galoot? It's his job to bring the cows in when Kate has a supper on. I don't know why she puts up with him—lazy, good-for-nothing. He's like a fly on a nun when there's work to do. Father was right to have as little to do with servants as possible. We never had dieters, and more often than not Father did his hand-lining alone. He said it was human nature for people to avoid extra work when they weren't likely to benefit from it, but it drove him wild to see anyone sitting around dreaming, so he usually managed to get by with just an old man or a boy for the fishing season.

We never had trouble getting good help then, not like now. It was Mother's cooking, I know that. She was such a good manager, and since Father ate his dinner down with the help she always gave them the best she could manage, within reason. They knew that when they signed on. In some places, the servants were half starved, given maggoty fish and fousty biscuit all summer, so it was inevitable that they'd drink themselves to sleep whenever they could get their hands on a bottle. Not in our rooms, though. As long as I could remember, Father always managed to get Mother the little extras that made cooking the same food over and over again a bit easier—mustard seed and nutmeg, quills of cinnamon bark, and cider for making vinegar.

It didn't take much then to make a servant happy. We had a hop-pole in the back, for making bread as a change from biscuit, and a little beer for special occasions. There was native mint up by the well, and I used to walk on it deliberately when I went to get water so that I could sniff it in at every step back to the house. And the savory from the garden—oh, the smell of the savoury drying by the stove was heaven itself.

That Big Galoot Kate hired is fed like a king and is lazy as a cut cat. Still, he's a decent enough man, I suppose, not like that sleeveen Thomas Salter. I'll never understand how Father came to take him on—probably felt sorry for him. Mother, too. Mother seemed to like him well enough. I never took to him— I could smell a villain from the moment he walked into the house. What other summer servant ever came into the house? Thomas Salter was a sly one, always some excuse to come sniffing around the kitchen, looking for extra handouts. I have to confess, I thought it was Mother he was after. Maybe it was, and I . . . no, don't blame yourself. That would be like blaming Lizzie if the Big Galoot . . . Oh, Sweet Gentle Joseph, surely he wouldn't ever touch Lizzie.

It's hard lying in this bed all day, with too much time to think. I'm starting to imagine problems that don't exist. I should remember only the good times, not the bad ones, the way Mr. Donovan taught me, but it's not in my nature. Like the cats, for instance. Cats were needed on every fishing premise to prevent the rats cutting up the nets and trawl lines, and we girls had such fun with them, babying them and putting them up in swaddling and bonnets. But when I think of the cats, foremost in my mind is the time I found that Thomas Salter had taken two young toms and tied their tails together and slung them over the line that Father used for drying rounders. They ate one another alive, and there was nothing I could do because they wouldn't stop their biting and clawing long enough for me to get them down. Finally I cut the line and let the dogs finish them off, but I could never again take pleasure in seeing a sweet little moggie being crooned to sleep in some child's arms.

Later that August I was out behind the Harbour, far back by the river, cutting country hay by the banks with a little grass hook. The whorts still weren't really ripe and I was restless to get at them, so Mother sent me to cut the wild grasses by the river. I'd been at it for hours, and had stopped to sharpen the hook on a little bit of grindstone Father had given me that had broken off his. He'd shown me how to keep the edge on the blade, to make the work easier. It was hot so I'd taken off my shoes and stockings and when the blade was sharp I started picking over the low berry bushes, just for a spell, finding a few ripe berries to bring home to Father for his evening lunch. I didn't hear anything, what with the noise of the river and the blood pounding in my ears from being so hot, and all of a sudden someone caught hold of my bare foot and pulled me backwards onto my face. Oh, the dirty man, I can feel the flush on my face now, his fingers up my skirts, poking and probing at my privates.

I heard my father say to Mother that I probably didn't know what he was trying to do to me, but I knew. You'd see it all the time under the flakes, the wolfish dogs going at it all the time, and the bad girls down there with the store clerks from Newman's. I was screeching and I could hear him laughing, and the berries all over the grass under me. I never did get the stains out of that pinafore. I took the bit of frill off and used the rest of it for rags after, and every time I mopped up a bit of spilt tea or a drip from the molasses keg I imagined I was wiping Thomas Salter's name off the face of the earth.

The worst was I managed to forget for a time, and then

when I married Paddy it all came back, he was so clumsy and stupid, grabbing at me like I was some kind of streel off the back streets. There were times I thought I might do to Paddy what I did to Thomas Salter. He got hold of my drawers, and I fought, hanging on to them through my skirts, and then I just let go and scraveled away, leaving the garment in his hands, and I went on my hands and knees for the river and suddenly the grasshook was under my hand and . . .

Why didn't he stop? If he'd dropped the drawers and just gone on I'd have told no-one, but I couldn't go home without them. None of us had more than one change of clothes, not even underthings, and I had to have them back. He laughed at me. He held them up to his nose and said dirty things and laughed at me, and the handle of the hook was there under my fingers, hidden in the grass, and I was crying, snot running down my face, and I begged him to give them back but he taunted me.

Why did he get so close? I was aiming for his eyes, those dirty, pale blue eyes that saw everything under my skirts, and he flung his hand up to stop it. There was a big slash through the drawers, and the whole thumb gone, so they knew he'd had them in his hand when I cut him, knew I was telling the truth. One of his friends got him out of the Harbour on board a boat to St. Pierre before the magistrate arrived. I was eleven years old. I never had any trouble with the boys after that.

We didn't talk about it outside the house, nor inside it after Thomas Salter was gone from the Harbour. I told my parents he never did anything except put his dirty fingers up my skirts—I imagine that thumb rotted in the grass out by the river—but I think people supposed more had happened, for no respectable boy ever came courting me in later years, not even though girls were so few and my parents were ready to do anything they could for me when I married. Perhaps that's why the Bishop stepped in, sent Paddy Aylward from town to meet me, almost the last thing he did before he put aside this mortal coil. Paddy said the Bishop gave him assurances I was a good girl, but once, when he was in his cups, he admitted he thought the Bishop was as capable of lying for a good cause as any man.

Was I a good cause? I tried my best, but Paddy just didn't know how to approach a woman, not unless she was a trollop from the back streets with a belly full of grog and half a dozen bastard children traipsing behind her. Paddy wasn't a bad man, not like Thomas Salter, but he wasn't a good man like Mr. Donovan, either. I can't even wish he'd been different, because he could never have been different enough to please me.

I mind the first time I saw Paddy, he was standing in the doorway, looking like the very corner boy, decked out in a snuff-brown coat reaching to his ankles. The coat had been made from a worn greatcoat of his uncle's, and was still miles too big for him, and on his head was a white hat that was battered in the sides and crown. That white hat—it was completely ridiculous, and I blushed every time I saw it coming down the path from town. Maybe I married Paddy to save him from that nonsensical white hat. One of the first things I did once we were man and wife was to lose that hat in the bottom of a dead-man's chest in the kitchen. He was searching for it for months, lamenting losing such an invaluble and attractive head-covering. Serves me right for being embarrassed by him—there are more important things than clothes, as I keep telling Lizzie, and you should never be embarrassed by anybody's behavior but your own.

He was an odd looking character, was Paddy—small and wiry, with a mop of frizzy yellow hair and a big mouth. He was rough, more like a sailor in his clothes and manner than like a respectable tradesman, and always hot-tempered, irascible and loud by nature, and profane in language—you could see the sulphur coming out his ears when he got his dander up. Still and all, most men thought him a clever sort, what they called a good fellow or a card, and most women were far from immune to his charm, though it managed to escape me for most of our married life. Poor Paddy; it must be hard to be married to a woman who doesn't like you very much, however obedient she is.

He told me once I'd as much flavour as the white of an egg, yet in my own defence I know that, insipid as it is, the egg is good for little but glue if it hasn't the white. Now that I think of it, if I was like the white, Paddy was like the yolk—concentrated, colourful, too strong in flavour and too thick in consistency, just begging to be thinned or leavened by the white. He was the life of any gathering, and our kitchen was always full of people having a good time, but it was me who prepared the food and cleaned up the mess after. It's a poor party you'd have on an empty stomach.

One thing Paddy could do was make a first-rate boot, though if he hadn't had me to run the business end of things, it would have been a mess in no time at all. I'd learned my lessons from Father and Mother, and I have echoed their voices time and again in passing on that wisdom to my own children. "A few dollars paid cash over the counter means a considerable saving at any time." "Local or Spanish, coin will buy more than trade." "Truck will lead to debt, and credit will lead to disaster." "Disbursments must never exceed earnings." "Take in more than you lay out." "Never eat your bread before you've earned it." Paddy had to be watched, because if he had one copper in his pocket and another at home in the Labrador box, he would spend both of them twice. He worked hard when he worked, and he turned a good dollar in his day, but it was always feast or famine.

Trying to keep Paddy confined in the store was like trying to keep a frog in a barrel—he was always leaping up and rushing out to the nearby shops to purchase some small item, or checking the weather or running some errand. No room was big enough to hold him, and in winter it seemed as if he were constantly bouncing off the walls. Even when he sat as still as a stone, when he was listening to an elaborate story or a fine old ballad being sung by some visitor, you had the sense that he was quivering inside, that he was coiled to bound upward and outward. Paddy Beg, many people called him, because he was small, but more often he would be called Springheeled Jackson, for he seemed to have springs in his shoes. Perhaps he really did, for he could make a shoe that made a short man tall, or a crippled girl straight, or a clumsy child nimble and graceful. Paddy could work miracles with his clicker and his last.

Mother used to say that the greatest miracle in the Bible was revealed to us when God reminded us in Deuteronomy that after forty years wandering the desert, "Thy shoe is not waxen old upon thy foot." To think of all those people, walking and walking for forty years, and the shoes grew on the feet of the children and never broke or wore out. A miracle indeed, and not one we were blessed with. When I was a child, it was my mother who kept the shoes on our feet from becoming old, and indeed rotting off them, for Father never acquired the knack of waxing up the hempen cord to make the tacker for harnesses and shoes. Paddy could do it blindfolded, or blind drunk even, but Father couldn't get the wax to stick and he just couldn't manage the meticulous, tiny stitches the boots and harnesses needed, which is perhaps why he was so impressed by Paddy that he almost paid him to take me.

Newfoundland is a hard climate for a bad boot—a shoddy piece of work means chilblains, frostbite, cracked and swollen heels, and toes with the nails falling off. Half the children in the Harbour were crippled from having bad boots or no boots at all. We had no logans then, no rubber boots, and the mud and wet and salt water was hard on footwear, so Mother cared for our boots, setting up the little last on the table in the evening and tapping the sprigs in, trimming down the leather for new soles or carefully detaching the topsides to construct an almost new pair from old ones. And always and ever she was greasing them up, scooping up the dark yellow muck and working it into every seam, every stitch, every crack of the leather. She said it kept her own hands softer, made it easier for her to hold a needle after a day on the flakes.

Paddy made a good boot, that's certain. No matter what condition he was in, when he had the leather in his hand he could make up a blucher or what we called a half gallon in no time at all. When we first had the shop near Springdale Street, he would sell the shoes right off our feet, calling the children in from their games, or me from the back linney, and then he would sit down and make a new pair as quick as a wink. He could make anything from a strong fishermen's boot to a lady's fine drawing room shoe, and make it as good as any Hamburg cordwainer. A pair of bluchers with swanskin or buskins were about the tidiest, warmest and most comfortable cover any man could put on his foot.

Paddy had a sign in the window, over a pair of sample bluchers: "We never claim they are waterproof but they oblige the foot of man, woman or child in every other way." The first sign he made said that his boots would keep the feet of Pharaoh's army dry, but I made him take it down as it was a lie, and possibly even blasphemous, so we compromised with the other. I never could understand why Paddy, who made one of the best boots at a reasonable price in the entire colony, could not just be satisfied with the truth but had to layer it over with a lie every time.

I recall once Paddy had promised a pair of boots to a fellow from the Garrison, but one of the apprentices sliced his hand on a knife, nearly taking off his finger, and it was Paddy sat with the boy one whole weekend, keeping the hand still and soaking the infection out. I had the girls down with measles at the time and it wasn't a bad case but they needed constant tending and I just couldn't leave them, so Paddy sat two nights with the boy and probably saved his arm at the very least. When the officer came in on Monday to get his boots, Paddy was shaking from loss of sleep and had eyes like two burnt holes in a blanket. He could hardly hold an awl, let alone turn out a pair of first-rate boots in a morning, so he made up some bit of nonsense about the leather being unavailable and the Spanish ship his order was on going down off Majorca. The officer was furious—it was so obviously all a lie. You could see the judgment written in his eyes, and as he went through the door I heard him say "Sot!" under his breath.

I asked Paddy after why he didn't just tell him the truth, that he'd been nursing the boy all weekend which was nothing to be ashamed of, and he said he hadn't thought quick enough. That was Paddy's burden, and mine; the truth always came to his tongue a second or two slower than a lie. I don't know where he got this from—Old Mr. Fitzgibbon, who's been dead this sixty years, told me that he knew Paddy's family in Kilkenny, and was on the wharf there the day Paddy sailed for America. He came from respectable people—his father was a crippled man who kept a store, a dry-goods shop of some sort—but he just couldn't stick to the truth, and it drove me wild. If he sold twenty pairs of boots, he said it was thirty. If he had four men working for him, or six, he said it was eight or ten. He claimed to be doing so well that he was constantly being asked for small loans and donations, and since he wouldn't admit he hadn't the coin, he'd rob the few dollars I kept for emergencies in the lustreware jug and just give it away to anyone who told a lie as well as he did himself.

Paddy was so open-fisted, such a braggart, that it was rumored he'd found a crock of gold in the back yard when he was building the foundation for our back linney. The only crock of gold he ever found was me, for I managed to stretch a penny to a pound, and it was Father's money that built the shop in the first place, for he never doubted for a moment that every word that came out of Paddy Aylward's mouth was as true as Holy Writ. Father saw the shop as income for his old age, when he would come and live with me and Paddy and watch our children grow up as he grew old, and Paddy would see that none of us ever wanted for a thing. It didn't quite work out that way— Father never got old enough to stop fishing, and Paddy never saw the girls grow up, but if he had I don't doubt we would have been less than wealthy.

After Paddy died, I sold the premises just in time; the building was rented but I got $5,000 for the heavy machinery, $950 for the light machinery, utensils and appliances, and $1,900 for the on-hand stock of leather and semi-finished materials. The company who bought me out promised jobs for seven men and one boy, and by the time I had paid all the outstanding debts as well as the funeral and the tabs Paddy ran at the various she-beens around town, most of the money was gone but I still had enough to buy the farm out in the Waterford Valley. If Paddy had died two years later, we'd have been lucky to get half that price, for the factories were taking over and the logans and rubber boots were just coming onto the island. I got us out just in time.

The cows are coming in now. I wish Kate had someone to count on. I'd never wish a man like Paddy on her, for he was too unpredictable, and it's the not-knowing that's the worst. But if he was managed properly, even the Big Galoot could be company for her, some sort of comfort. Here, Paddy has been dead now longer than he was ever alive, and he still lives with me. I find his yellow hair in the butter, and I can hear his heels banging on the floor as I am falling asleep at night. The only time I could ever escape him was when Mr. Donovan wrapped his big, heavy arms around me and his warm breath on the top of my head would drive all thoughts of Paddy out of my memory for minutes and hours at a time. And now, here I am remembering the energy and the clever hands almost as if I had loved him once. I never loved him—I never loved anyone until I loved my own sweet man. Kate is better off with no-one than with the likes of Paddy Aylward.

June 11

Stephen Walsh's brother-in-law was here, asking if I'd sell the hotel. Said he figured I couldn't manage on my own and acted like he was doing me a favour to take it off my hands. The face of him, and Mumma upstairs probably hearing every word. I told him I wasn't on my own and it isn't my hotel to sell. Dropped and broke the large pudding bowl in cleaning it. Fine day.

*L*izzie was here, talking to amuse me. She says she has proof positive that Mr. Delgado dyes his hair. She can be a wicked gossip, but she knows when to hold her tongue. There are certain professions that require discretion, and the hotel business is one of them. "Tell the truth, the half truth, and nothing like the truth," as Mr. Reid used to say. Sometimes I think it is the silent ones who learn most, for I'm lying here as dumb as a post and I'm learning all sorts of things I didn't know before. If I ever get my tongue to obey me again, I'll have a thing or two to tell Kate about that Annie in the kitchen.

Now Father was never one to gossip, yet his twine loft drew men from all over the Harbour in the off-season. I don't know why that would be—Father wasn't a talker, and though he had a pleasant word for most, he wasn't a particularly sociable man. He kept no beer or rum on the wharf and never tolerated those who brought it with them, nor did he smoke although he didn't object to those who did. I suppose he had a dour and taciturn nature, a congenitally gloomy outlook on life. I recall once when Mother was feeling particularly optimistic about the outcome of some enterprise, a new cow or some hardy potato stock perhaps, Father kept reining her back with predictions of disaster until, in frustration, she stamped off to the other room and returned with the Bible which she thrust into his hands with the suggestion that he read the Book of Job to cheer himself up.

Father's dark, quiet moods seemed, if anything, to attract other men to him. When they arrived at his rooms, they would insinuate themselves into the gloom of the shed, finding a corner out of his way, and after a time they would begin to talk. He listened, I suppose, but it's hard to say—perhaps he didn't. Often these visitors picked up a bit of net or some item that needed work and would set to repairing it, often holding it out to Father to check that he approved or to accept direction, for if it was not done to standard Father would simply lay the object to one side, and the next time they came it would have been redone properly. He worked relentlessly, but he did it with an economy of movement that made it soothing rather than enervating, and the pace he set at the beginning of the morning was maintained right up to the moment he stopped work for the day.

The fire in the twine loft chimney burned only when there was reason—if nets had to be mended, a fire was necessary to keep fingers from becoming stiff and clumsy. Barking and ironwork was done out of doors, but pots of glue, tar, seal oil with ochre, things related to work rather than food, were heated on the flat sheet of iron that could be slid over the grating of the twine loft chimney. Occasionally food was cooked there also. Sometimes we children would gather huge buckets of mussels that would be boiled in sea water and kelp in the twine loft, and the men would shell and beard them as they talked quietly among themselves, eating at least as many as they tossed into the crock that Mother would eventually top-up with vinegar and mustard seed and seal with wax for the coming Christmas season. I once burned the corner of my apron by using it to move a glue pot, and was so mortified by the scolding Mother gave me that I threw the scorched garment down the privy hole—Richard hooked it out with a gaff, and I had to scrub the filthy thing until it gleamed white again, and then resew it for a neighbour's smaller child. Mother didn't think the twine loft was a good place for a girl.

Sometimes one of the regulars would bring a fish or a half dozen herring which they would boil up with a bit of Hamburg biscuit that Father kept in a string bag next to the chimney. I rarely took part in these impromptu lunches but Richard would tell me about them. Once I was present when someone brought a halibut. I was thrilled to the ends of my hair when it was served out on platters of spruce shingle, for we ate it with our fingers which would never have been allowed up at the house. Almost everyone smoked except Father, so there was often a strong scent of tobacco or tar or seaweed to cut through the ever-present odour of salt fish and gurry that permeated the place. In the deep of winter, the twine lofts were where the men went to escape the oppressive domesticity of the houses, with their bawling babies, steaming kettles and harried women. Work at these times was a relief to the men, who did not know how to savour their few idle hours the way the women did. Richard virtually lived in the twine loft in winter.

Richard had the fisherman's instinct from the day he was born. I recall one beautiful May morning, when he was about five years old and I was perhaps nine, we were down near the shore at Maddox Cove poking about where someone had pulled a boom of spruce logs in to the beach to begin building a stage. I don't recall what had drawn us there but Mother had warned us to stay away from the logs, which were unstable in the water and when stepped on were likely to flip upward and knock out an unwary child. Richard could not be kept from the shore for long, and I was trying to distract him by collecting tiny starfish which we were laying out on a flat rock in the form of the big dipper and the other constellations that we recognized. Suddenly, there was a commotion in the water and before I could stop him, Richard was in among the logs, up to his waist in water.

I don't know what I thought it was—a mermaid perhaps. There was often talk of mermaids at school, but they were generally thought to inhabit the shore waters only when there was ice about. I suppose they were invented by our mothers to keep us off the water at such dangerous times. It was said that the mermaids would pull you into the water from the pans and cut your legs off and give you a tail, and they would never give you anything to eat but sea lice and guffies. When I heard this mighty splash and saw the silver tail flinging water everywhere, I naturally thought it was a mermaid and was sure she had come to carry Richard out to sea. Richard had no such fancies, however—he recognized a salmon when he saw one, for Father used to occasionally get them and would split them, pickle them in brine and pack them in barrels for sale in St. John's.

What ructions we kicked up—Richard grabbing for the salmon which was trapped in the shallow water by the logs, me grabbing for Richard, the slippery stones underfoot making every step a menace. Somehow, he managed to push the salmon up onto the beach so that I could see it really was only an ordinary fish, though the knife-like fins made it seem like some sort of glorious sea-monster, almost as exotic as a mermaid. Planting his feet securely into the shingle, Richard prevented the creature from regaining the water, but it was so slick and wet that it was impossible to get a grip on it and even with my help he was unable to move it much further up the beach. Turning to me in despair, and by this time panting with effort, he shouted "Take off your dress, Kezzy. Take it off, now."

Fortunately, it being so early in the year, I was wearing a petticoat or Richard would have had me stripped to my skin, so determined was he to keep that salmon. The apron came off, and then the dress, and in a very short time we had our catch slung into the skirts of my homespun shift. By the time we got the fish to the top of the hill over Petty Harbour we were both dropping with fatigue, but fortunately Father had come in search of us and relieved us of our burden. Mother was not pleased to see me arrive home half-naked, nor was she delighted to see my only dress tied around the salmon by my apron strings, but Richard's pride and pleasure was such that once she had extracted a promise that we would never do such a thing again, she gave herself up to the excitement of the moment.

The salmon must have weighed ten pounds at least, and although we normally had our main meal in the middle of the day and made do with a cold lunch in the evening, Mother cooked the tail in a piece of muslin and served it up to us with a creamed mustard sauce and boiled potatoes. Richard didn't manage to get more than a few mouthfuls down his throat before falling asleep over his plate, but Father ate every mouthful of his own as well as Richard's leftovers, and before going to sleep that night he salted down the remainder, which we ate on special occasions throughout the winter. Mother made me wash the dress and apron myself, and since it rained the next day I was forced to wear one of her work dresses, which was so worn it had recently been consigned to the matting bag in the rafters. It was, however, a small price to pay for the intense pleasure Richard derived from his first major catch.

Lizzie used to ask me, when she was small, if I'd had a best friend when I was a girl and would give me her hard, skeptical look when I answered that perhaps my brother was my best friend. Lizzie hardly even looks at her brother, and acts as if time spent with him is a peculiar form of torture. My childhood wasn't like hers. I hardly ever played structured games, nor did many of the children in the Harbour. I used to watch my own girls play hopscotch and jackstones as if they were savages from across the water in Africa, so foreign were these things to me.

Lizzie was right, of course—Richard and I weren't friends, but we were one another's closest companions, not counting Mother and Father. Perhaps it was because we all worked so hard that there was little time for friendships, or perhaps it was because we were solitary by nature, but neither of us sought out the company of other children, and they rarely sought ours. Mother didn't encourage visiting, for we often had a difficult enough time feeding and clothing ourselves without having half-starved and ragged children from around the Harbour hanging in the doorway making hungry eyes at our few possessions.

Since we lived on the Southside but attended school and church on the Northside, we didn't mix much with the neighbours, except perhaps when there was an illness or death to be dealt with. At such times, Richard might be sent with an armload of wood or I might be told to mind a small child for a few hours, but like everyone we had limited resources and barely enough energy to keep body and soul together given the short season for fishing and gardening. Mother used to say that it was just as well our summers weren't longer as we would wear our bodies out well before their time. Winter came almost as a relief, for once the snow was down there was little to do but stay warm and seek relief from the boredom of long, dark days by fashioning the few small comforts we could create for ourselves.

In summer, there were not enough hours in the day to do all that had to be done. Aside from the endless task of making the fish, there was the garden to be seen to. We always struggled to find time for chinching the house, mending the roof and the hundred other chores that could only be done in reasonably good weather. It was my responsibility to gather the hop-buds before they blew, to pinch the young leaves of the Indian tea and dry them over the stove, haul seaweed and gurry to the garden, gather moss and country hay, mind the goats, keep the water bucket full, and much more. Once the garden was done, I had to pick partridgeberries and bounceberries, help slaughter the goats . . . Oh, the list is endless. The hours together when my own girls played with dolls or pretended to mind a shop were not something I had ever experienced.

I do recall occasional times of idleness, but they were rare. Father had acquired a dog soon after he came to this country, a big, sweet-natured water dog he called Egypt, and I believe Egypt was my playmate for some time. I remember my mother telling me that when I first learned to walk, I would make my way down with her to the flakes by holding onto Egypt's ears and staggering along the rough path from the house. He used to fish for guffies next to the wharf—I'd be sitting on a rock watching him take one after another of the ugly creatures and drop them into a pile at my mother's feet. I don't recall he ever ate them, but I expect they went into the garden with the caplin and the gurry.

The shoreline at Petty Harbour is so steep, and frontage so scarce, that every square inch is needed for the fish. The broad flakes are in some places eight and ten feet high over the water, and I occasionally used to go under them with Egypt. I rarely dared go there without him, for this was the domain of the many wolfish dogs that infested the Harbour—dogs that had no proper owners or were abused by the men who laid claim to their labour.

I have to this day a mortal fear of most dogs, for once I saw a pack of these brutes tear the scalp off a small boy. He was perhaps four years old, and what I was doing there under the flakes I can no longer recall, except that I was poking at a pile of maggots with a stick and looked up just as he took a misstep and fell. The moment he was down, the dogs were on top him. I never knew the boy to speak to him but I often saw him in later years, his head topped with a few comical tufts of hair and covered in a patchwork quilt of scars where his mother had pulled the skin back from his face and neck and stitched a cover for his bare skull. She claimed to have cured him by putting sluts on the wounds—nine female puppies, one slit open each day and applied fresh to his scalp nine days in a row.

Richard must have been with my father the day I saw the child scalped, for unlike me he was a fine natural sailor and enjoyed being on the water. Once Richard was old enough to take his place in the skiff, Egypt came to work with me in the garden, pulling stones, hauling waste for fertilizer, applying his patience and muscle to a myriad of dreary chores. In winter he hauled wood and water, and in summer it was seaweed and gurry, and in all seasons he protected us from the wild dogs that ran in packs around the Harbour. When he got old and rheumatic, he still struggled to do the work of a whole army of dogs and it broke my heart to see him lurching stiff-legged after Richard or Father when they went on the water. I suppose I looked at Egypt the way Kate looks at me now.

One day Father lifted Egypt into the boat, and I saw his nose and his tail tilt up in delight as the boat moved out the Harbour, but Father came back without him. He told us that Egypt had seen a puffin and had leapt from the boat and swum away, but Richard told me that the small killick was gone too, and we knew what had happened. When winter came, Father bought a pony from a man who had no hay to feed it.

Paddy wasn't fond of dogs—his incessant gatching and teasing earned him more than one nip at his heels from the crackies and water dogs in the town, and if he'd drink taken he was likely to strike a preliminary defensive blow with the toe of his boot. I have never been able to stomach the violent ways so many men have with their animals. I've seen the boys baiting fish hooks to catch gulls, and then after they've pulled half their guts out through their mouths they cut the legs off the poor creatures and leave them to die slowly. A boy who will do that is bound to turn into a man who will abuse his wife and children.

I have never owned a dog since I had Egypt, though I have worked with any number of ponies and horses and have yet to own one that could do half the work of Egypt in his prime. I was glad Father had drowned Egypt, for other men were not so kind and would kill an old dog with a blow from an axe, and do it badly. Then they'd take the skin and leave the carcass to the crows and gulls, which seems poor reward for all their hard work—a few shovels full of dirt to cover them seems little enough to ask. If we can't give an animal a good life, the least we can offer is a quick and humane death. I've never seen any point in drawing out any creature's suffering.

June 17

Mauzy day. Too early for caplin but took the train over to Topsail Beach with Dermot just to look. I was tired when we left but he coaxed me into it and I felt quite exhilarated by the time we returned home. I guess it is all the fresh air. Met Monsignor Roche on the way, and addressed him as Father in error, which earned me a poke from Dermot who does it on purpose all the time, just to annoy him. He is so young it's easy to forget. Mumma seems a little better.

Kate came in smelling of the sea. She had been down to Topsail and helped Mrs. Atkins turn the fish on the flakes. Kate hasn't much colour usually, but today with her hair blown about and the flush on her cheeks, she looked very pretty. I always think of Kate as belonging in the dairy, just as I have always belonged in the kitchen, but she surprised me today by saying she enjoyed making the fish. She must have been telling the truth, for it can't have been the company of that galoot Dermot that made her look so lively. I wouldn't have thought an afternoon spent breaking your back was anything to speak fondly of.

I never liked making fish and I was glad not to have to do it. It would seem to be impossible to grow up in Petty Harbour and not be engaged in the fishery but I was the rare exception, and as I have never loved the sea or anything related to her I am not sorry. My education in the fishery began the summer after the smallpox epidemic and came to a premature end the following year. My mother, frightened by how helpless I had been before the Bishop arrived, and perhaps impressed by how well I worked under his tuition, determined that my infancy was at an end and my initiation into this vale of tears should begin as soon as possible. Such a determination sounds harsher than it was—at that time, children who could barely walk or feed themselves were expected to help make fish, and my childhood had been unusually prolonged in that no demands had ever been made of me in that direction.

As I was only six, and greener than most children that age, I had little to do but watch that first season. My mother would call me when she went to the flakes and would explain what she was doing and why. The fish had to be stacked, spread, covered, uncovered, turned and gathered in endless combination, all with a view to drying it out without burning it with too much sun or salt or wind. Mother would direct my attention skyward a dozen times a day and point out cloud formations. Then she would direct my eyes to the branch of a tree or bush and have me determine the wind direction. From indications such as these, we had to decide whether we could spread the fish on the flakes, or whether they should be turned, covered or gathered in to be transferred to the sheds on hand barrows.

The weather was an obsession with all of those engaged in catching or making fish. Are the cows lying down? Is the soot falling in the chimney? Do the hills seem too close? Are the birds feeding or perching? One of the first Bible verses I learned to read entirely by myself was Matthew 16: 2 and 3.

Our Lord said to the Pharisees, "When it is evening, ye say it will be fair weather for the sky is red, and in the morning it will be foul weather today, for the sky is red and lowering. Oh ye

hypocrites, ye can discern the face of the sky
but can ye not discern the signs of the times?"

Mother had a keen nose, and if she could smell the earth closet, which was below the house over a small ditch, she was alert for rain and we were on tenterhooks. Even my own behavior was taken into account. One morning, Richard and I were loud and rackety, inclined to giggles over our breakfast, and she got very uneasy and a little sharp with us. She walked down to the flakes with Father, to study the sky before he took his boat out for the second trip of the day, and everything looked like fair weather so he went about his work, but just before she came into the house, the cow up in the field flicked its tail three times and took a kick at a rabbit or something. Then, as she stepped through the door, Richard upset a pan of milk warming on the stove. She didn't even stop to clean the milk up—left it to burn and ran with all her might down to the wharf again to call Father back in off the water. An hour later, it was blowing a gale and a bait skiff went down with all hands drowned.

The labour of spreading, turning and gathering the fish was endless, and there were few short cuts. If only a shower was expected, it was sometimes judged appropriate merely to turn the fish skin side up, but if any amount of rain at all was due, the fish had to be gathered in piles and covered with rinds or old sailcloth or anything to keep them dry. Serious weather required that the fish be put under proper cover and for this Mother had to have help, usually a boy or old man belonging to one of the bigger families, hired on through the summer in exchange for board alone.

Since the cod run in summer, the demands of the fishing season conflicted with those of the garden, yet Mother managed both almost cross-handed. Little wonder that she struggled so hard to get me to help her with the fish. It wasn't to be, however. I attended well enough when she was teaching me to notice what colour of blue or grey or purple lay upon the sea, and I am still all nerves when the horses start gailing, but the following year when it was necessary for me to dirty my hands more seriously, we both came up against an insurmountable impediment. The Bishop said that God never intended to engage me in the fishery, and let it go at that, but of course he had his eye on me for the schoolroom which I didn't take to either.

I had always been a healthy, sturdy child, as big at seven as most children were at nine or ten, and I have never shirked work, so I fell to with the fish willingly enough at first, but it took less than a week before my hands were cracked and red and swollen, and every day it seemed to get worse faster. There seemed to be something in the liquid which the salt drew out of the fish that I simply could not tolerate. All of the women had sore hands, covered in scars, blisters and calluses, just as all the men had pups around their wrists and lines through the palms of their hands where the twine cut in, but this was many degrees worse and I knew from the start that it was not going to go away. I tried for weeks, crying when I was alone and hiding my hands in my pinafore, but in a short time my poor paws were so swollen and bleeding that I couldn't hold a spoon to my mouth. Father could hardly bear to look at me, and I could see the tears spring into his eyes at times when he came home and silently lifted the clean cloth Mother used to cover my hands when she was treating them.

The day my nails began to fall off was the last day I worked at the fish. Mother had been soaking my hands in chamber lye, a common cure for what we used to call fish finger, and the pain was so extreme that I fought away from her and she had to bind my arms to my sides with a piece of rope in order to hold my hands down in the liquid. I had managed to kick the pot over onto the two of us. Father came in just then and found us sobbing at the kitchen table, me tied up in Mother's lap and the two of us covered in Richard's urine while Richard crouched in a corner watching the process with big, dark eyes. Despite his age, he had wet himself with fright so we were all soaked and reeking.

"Enough," Father said, and that was that. He disappeared out the door and I think it was with relief that Mother gave in without a word. By the time we were all cleaned up and changed into our dry clothes, Father was back with a small pannikin which he warmed over the kitchen stove. It held a tarry, black mixture softened with cod liver oil, and he spread it over my hands and bound them loosely in strips of cloth. For a week, he and Mother took turns feeding me, lifting my nightdress so I could use the pot, reading to me from the Bible, and at the end of the week when Father gently removed the tar with more of the oil, my hands were almost their normal size and colour.

Thus began my training as a farmer. Even before my nails grew back, I had taken the mattock and climbed the hill behind our house to the gardens my mother kept, and gave the weeds and worms a blow for every fish my mother turned. Sometimes, when it was an emergency and the fish were almost dry, I would help with turning or stacking, but Father hated to see me near the flakes and Richard claimed the entire wharf and flake area as his own territory, sometimes even throwing stones at me from behind a barrel to drive me away. Soon he was the one my mother turned to when the sky threatened. Richard was born to the fishery just as surely as I wasn't.

That October, after the seasonal fishermen left, I began school. It came as something of a shock to discover that I wouldn't be going to Mistress Martin on the Southside, but to Miss Lacey at the Northside school. Looking back at it, I think it was just as well, for Master Martin would have had all the baptismal records from the Anglican Church and would have known my exact age, while Miss Lacey guessed that I was three years older than I was and treated me accordingly. Most of the Irish were illiterate and didn't know their numbers, so when they were asked the date of their birth they answered "Feast of Our Lady of the Pillar" and Miss Lacey would consult her calendar and write down October 12th, or "Our Lady of Good Council"— July 10th, or in many cases "Two days after Sheila's Day" or "Bonfire Night less a week" for which even Miss Lacey didn't need a calendar. A year might be identified by the sinking of a ship or a forest fire, but generally Miss Lacey just guessed according to the size of the child.

When Mother gave my birth date as March 12th, Miss Lacey glanced up at me, declared "And she'd be ten, I suppose." I opened my mouth to protest, but my mother's hand on my shoulder warned me to be quiet, and instead of correcting her, my mother simply added the information that I could read already. Miss Lacey looked quite cheered at this news, probably because, as I realized some years later, she was not too confident in this area herself. I suppose she was all of sixteen.

I soon found myself placed at a bench next to two older girls I knew only by sight, but within a day or two I found that I was more teacher than student. Most of the bigger boys and many of the girls didn't attend school in the morning, but helped their parents with the fishing and such, but my mother insisted I be at my bench when the bell rang. The morning class was usually full of small children, who were inclined to fall asleep over their dinners and miss the afternoon sessions, so I was employed during those hours in doing alphabets and simple exercises with the small ones while Miss Lacey struggled to beat a little education into the older children. The beating process was literal—she used the strap frequently and indiscriminately, even on me at times, although I was a quiet and obedient pupil.

Our school room was plain but adequate—better than many I heard about later. We had several primers, and slates that

Father salvaged from a fire in St. John's that had destroyed a merchant's house. We had a good supply of rather hard chalk that had been collected by a Northside fisherman who had been swept away in a fog and stranded up the coast at Freshwater Bay for three days. The chalk required frequent spitting, which in turn required frequent visits to the water barrel, and eventually numerous trips to the outhouse, but all this activity prevented the most restless boys from rearranging one another's faces with their fists, so it was all to the good.

In winter the school was heated with a small stove that we fed with the two junks brought by each of us every morning. Sometimes we would be given a load of peat from down the coast, and if it were dry it would burn longer than the wood and produce a more even heat, but the fine, light ash was inclined to spread throughout the room from the drafts and settle in a thick, grey layer on every surface, so that even the best behaved students couldn't resist blowing it up one another's noses. When it got very cold, or the snow piled up over our heads, school was simply canceled. Lessons were scheduled to be conducted about six months out of the year, but we probably made it to our benches only about half that time.

I learned very little that was new in those first two years, but by teaching the smaller ones—as well as some of the bigger children, who were too dull even for Miss Lacey's simple lessons—I became more secure about my own grasp of the essentials of reading and writing. When Miss Lacey resigned to marry a middle-aged widower with half a dozen children, at least two of whom were older than she was herself, the four or five young men who succeeded her were happy to concentrate on teaching me the basic elements of addition, subtraction and multiplication in exchange for being allowed to abnegate all responsibility for the children under seven years of age. From then on, the baby classes were, for all intents and purposes, in my charge.

Many of the children never really did learn to read, though they could puzzle out a word or phrase. They could read the labels on boxes and barrels, but as often as not it was more an informed guess than an actual deciphering of the letters. My parents, being relatively comfortable with print, were frequently called upon to read letters that had come from Ireland or England for the Harbour families, and our precious hoard of cold-pressed whale or seal oil was often squandered while they painstakingly composed replies to these announcements of death, debt and disaster.

This unofficial service to the community only served to put a larger distance between us and our fellow communicants. We were privy to their secret disappointments, and they found that easier to accept if they thought of us as belonging to a slightly higher class of people than themselves, so the childen called me "teacher," even though I was a pupil like themselves, and my parents were called Mister and Missus, never Uncle or Aunt like many others. No money ever changed hands, for none of us had coin, nor was there ever an offer of goods for little as we had, we had more than most. But if someone asked me or my parents to read or write a letter, we would usually find them unexpectedly at hand and willing to help if there was seaweed to be hauled, or caplin to be ditched into the garden.

By the time I was fourteen years old, there was very little left for me to learn in the tiny Northside school and the Bishop suggested I go to school in town, to the Presentation sisters who had come over from Ireland to provide education to the girls of the colony. Bishop Fleming objected to having boys and girls in the same classroom because he felt it coarsened the girls. Even the smallest boys who worked in the fishery got a rum ration, and they often arrived for their lessons in a jolly and elevated mood that could quickly degenerate into lewd and obscene behavior, and since he couldn't stop them claiming their tot of

Jamaica, he felt the next best thing would be to remove the girls from their influence.

As far as I was concerned, separating the boys from the girls in school only put off the day when the girls would have to learn to cope with the problem, but my real objection was to leaving home, not to leaving behind a group of rowdy lads. The idea of going to town frightened me. As it happened, circumstances contrived to keep me at home for several more years, and by coaxing my mother into getting a second cow, I managed to make myself indispensable around the house. My mother had to make the fish and had no time to tend to the cows, and even went so far as to say she didn't want to since she had left all that behind in England, but at the same time she delighted in the increased variety that the butter and milk introduced into our very limited diet.

Salt pork and doughboys, salt beef and doughboys, salt fish and doughboys or biscuit, all accompanied by the potatoes, cabbage and turnips my mother and I wrestled out of the ever expanding garden on the hill behind the Harbour, was the best we could manage through the winter, and even at that we were luckier than most. To have butter for the fish, and milk to put in the morning tea, even if that tea was made from dried clover or marsh plants, was a luxury she had long since given up hope of seeing ever again.

The cows, I believe, lengthened my mother's life, forcing her to stay alive at least long enough to teach me how to milk, put by hay for the winter, and treat sore udders, not to mention how to churn butter and then wrap the pat in a fresh rhubarb leaf to set it, how to clean the pans so as to keep the liquid sweet and fresh in the root-cellar, and a dozen other skills that went far beyond mere milking. I was able to trade the milk and butter for an occasional fresh partridge or a haunch of the small caribou that roamed the interior of the island—almost hunted out now—and it meant that even when we had to hire on help to take Mother's place on the fish flakes, there was always some small, good thing to eat to coax a smile out of her right up to the day she passed out of this world and went to rest in the Bishop's cemetery until the morning of the Resurrection.

I know that my mother believed that as soon as she was gone, I would fulfill the Bishop's desire that I become a teacher, but there were things that happened at the school that I never told her about. Several of the young masters were brutes with the whip, and one of them in particular delighted in inflicting pain on the weakest and stupidest of the boys, though he left the girls pretty much to their own devices. One little fellow—he was from a particularly indigent family—took the brunt of this man's bottomless supply of anger, and something happened so that I felt compelled to go to the Bishop.

There had been talk of incest in the family—though nobody would have ever breathed the word—and certainly the child was odd, though not retarded in the usual sense. He had yellow, rheumy eyes and his nose was always running down to his chin and onto his smock, but aside from being a rather unappetizing boy, he wasn't so bad. The master, however, tormented him at every turn, making him kneel on pebbles for the slightest error and slapping him for "looking saucy." His favourite trick was to walk behind the children and rap the backs of their necks with a metal-trimmed ruler, claiming that if they were concentrating on their work it wouldn't hurt. That boy—Cajetan he was called—got so marked on the back of his neck that the scar tissue bunched and turned his head sideways, giving him an even more hangdog appearance.

One day I forgot my sampler in the school house and when I went back for it, I saw the master through the window beating poor Cajetan's bare bum with a ruler and rubbing the child over his knees in the most unholy way. I hammered at the door, though I don't think it was locked, and by the time I got into the room there was nothing but the child, snot and tears soaking his front. The ruler was back on the desk, streaked with blood. The master must have gone out the window.

That weekend, I coaxed Mother to let me go to town to bring the nuns some cranberry sauce she had made from berries I'd picked in the fall, and I managed to see the Bishop for a few minutes. I had never done such a bold thing in my life, and I was shaking like a leaf as I knocked on the door of his residence. I wasn't the only petitioner waiting on him that day, though I was certainly the youngest, but the moment I entered the room he knew something was weighing on me, for like many great men he had the ability to give his undivided attention, so that five minutes in his presence produced a feeling of satisfaction such as an hour or more with a less attentive person might.

"Keziah, my child, what is your trouble," he asked, as I bent to kiss his ring. I hardly knew how to answer. I could not tell him exactly what I had seen for I hardly understood it myself. He held my hand for a moment, and when I did not reply he gently lifted a finger under my chin so that my eyes met his. "Have I ever done anything to cause you to distrust me?" he asked.

"Oh no, Sir," I whispered, and tears came into my eyes at the thought that I might have offended him.

"Then you must trust me now, and tell me what is wrong," he responded.

"It's the master at the school, Sir. He is tormenting and beating the poor children so that they can hardly bear it." The tears turned to a torrent, and I wept openly at my own confusion and helplessness. "I cannot bear it myself, for just to watch is a torture." He looked grave and was silent for a moment.

"Keziah, you understand, do you not, that corporal punishment is a necessary and integral part of harnessing the human passions?" I did not answer, but continued crying and began searching frantically for my handkerchief in the basket I had at my side. "You have heard the saying, 'Spare the rod and spoil the child'?" he said less gently. With my handkerchief pressed to my face, I nodded. "Sometimes it is necessary to strike a child for his own good, and not to do so is a grave sin for it allows any weakness in the child's nature to take hold and grow."

"Oh, but Sir, the master is not doing it for the children, he is doing it for himself. He takes pleasure in hurting the little boys and they are so terrified that they cannot possibly learn." I scrubbed at my tears and determined to speak up on behalf of poor little Cajetan and the others.

"This is a serious accusation you are making, and not one that can be easily supported or disproven." The Bishop looked grim and angry now, but I did not feel he was angry at me. "If the masters and mistresses are to be of any use in the schools at all, they must be able to impose discipline where and when they feel it is necessary. You will discover that for yourself when you are a teacher with your own school."

"If being a teacher means I will have to break slates over the heads of my charges, or beat them until the blood runs down their legs, or terrify them so that the mere sight of me causes them to tremble, then I would rather see the whole nation remain in ignorance sooner than turn into such a person." If the Bishop was angry, I was beginning to feel some anger of my own. The Bishop sighed at my passionate outburst.

"Keziah, it is possible that some individuals lose control of the classroom and consequently lose control of themselves, but most masters are good men, under-educated perhaps, but attempting to do a difficult job for very little reward. Possibly this man goes a little too far, but you cannot throw out the whole system because it occasionally fails." He sighed again, and then gave me a rather sad smile. "We are old friends, you and I, and we should not be disagreeing in this way." I blushed at this, for it was dreadful temerity in me to disagree with the Bishop in any way at all. "I will look into the matter, but I also ask that you think this matter through, for when you are a teacher, you will need not just a knowledge of the alphabet and numbers, but a knowledge of human nature. Sometimes a lesson must be delivered with a blow if it is to be properly learned."

At that I knelt at his feet and he put his hands on my head and gave me his blessing but I resolved there and then never to be a teacher. The brutal master was removed and went on to two other schools before leaving the island in disgrace, and the boy Cajetan was put into my charge by the next master. I did my best to treat him with kindness, and at my urging Mother was able to get a few shillings from the church to clothe him properly. Poor little Cajetan—I suppose his parents gave him a fancy name as it didn't cost them anything. He shipped out of Petty Harbour as a catchee when he was eleven years old and I never heard of him again.

I have often wondered since if I should have been more forthright with the Bishop, but I was only fourteen and regardless of what I'd seen under the flakes in the evenings, I could not comprehend what I had witnessed. Instead, I turned my face away from the profession I was being trained for, and resolved never to use violence against any living being if I could avoid it. It is the one regret of my life that I broke that resolve.

June 22

Splendid day. Five tables of ladies for tea. Went to check on Mumma after lunch and found her with wet cheeks. Washed her face as gently as I could, and combed and rebraided her hair. She seems so sad today. Felt a little sad myself. I have spent my life being the baby, and now Mumma is the baby but I won't get to see her grow up.

Kate came and cleaned me up in case Father Roche should come, as he has so frequently in recent days. It was very soothing and after, she sat with the wet cloth in her hand and told me about how things were doing in the kitchen. The window was open, but that Big Galoot, Dermot, had forgotten to put the screen in so a nipper got into the room and bit Kate on the eye which was soon swollen half shut. The mark was so red and looked so painful on her pale face that I felt quite angry with Dermot, even after he brought her a fresh basin of water with a little soda in it to bath the eye. She scolded him, as she said I could have been eaten by the flies if it had not been such a breezy day, but I am never bitten. Too savoury, Mr. Donovan used to say to tease me.

Mother could never understand how it was that I could break out in blisters simply by looking at a bit of green fish, but I was apparently immune to fly bites. Father and Richard escaped them in early summer because they were on the water most of the time, but Mother had to stay with the fish on the flakes and she often finished her day dreadfully marked by the mosquitoes. The Bishop once jokingly called it the "Scourging at the Pillar" and said she should offer it up for the souls in Purgatory. She told Father later that when he said it, she wanted to answer that she'd do as well if she'd learned either to swear or to smoke, but came too late to do either and instead had to suffer the flies with nothing but a loop of oakum around her neck to drive them off.

Richard seemed to suffer even more than Mother from the hordes of mosquitoes that made life so difficult in June and July. If he was chopping wood, he would often set up a small smudge fire to keep them away, and old Egypt would crowd up against the pot with his head in the thick of the smoke, only to emerge in desperation some time later with red and streaming eyes. Up on the hill, in the gardens, I had the advantage of a breeze of wind to keep the flies from settling too often, but I also had my own way of coping with them. Like Mother, I always had a hank of oakum at hand, but in sultry weather this was of little use.

Caplin time was often the worst, for then the weather tended to be mauzy and the work could not be put off. At such times, the flies had to be ignored or no work would get done, so ignore them was what I did, though at times it was difficult. Regardless of the heat, I would bundle up with every extra bit of clothing I could find, more even than I might wear in winter, with the fringe of an old shawl dangling in my face to protect my eyes a little. Egypt would help me haul the caplin, which had to be turned into the earth before the maggots set in, and I'm afraid that good old dog suffered more than all the rest of us together.

At such times, I would apply what Richard had dubbed 'The Bishop's Holy Water,' which was water I collected from the pitcher plants in the bit of bog over past the river. During the smallpox outbreak, I had learned to gather this water in a little jug and strain it through a scrap of linen into a small bottle to apply to the eyes of the people who had the pox scabs on their faces. The Bishop feared that these poor sufferers would be left blind from the scarring on the eyes, and several times a day he would apply a few drops of this water from the handle of a spoon right into their eyes as a wash. Nobody in Petty Harbour was left blinded, so the application must have worked.

I would carry this water in a bottle in my pocket, and when poor Egypt's eyes and nose were a swollen mass of running sores from the flies, I would take a bit of well water and clean his face and then drop a bit of my precious "holy water" into his eyes, which were by then usually like two scarlet buttons in the black fur of his head. I would also drip a little over his poor swollen nose. He was generally very patient as I did this and seemed to know that it was for his own good, for he always sat quite still with his head in my lap. When I was done, I would drape a bit of brin sacking over his head and allow him to sleep for a short while before it was time to go down to the flakes and drag the gurry up to the garden as Mother took the fish from the splitting table for salting.

I asked the Bishop once why God who loves us would have put such fierce little creatures on earth to torture us, and he said it was to remind us of the millions of sins that daily lacerate His heart, and to turn our minds from evil to good by showing us how the Lord suffers on our behalf. But why then would an innocent creature such as Egypt be so plagued? And why would Richard, who was always cheerful and obedient, suffer so much more than me? For though I seemed quiet and accepting on the surface, in my heart I was stubborn and stiff-necked and both the Lord and I knew it, even if the Bishop and my parents didn't. I tolerated the mosquitoes because in my pride I wouldn't let them beat me, and so I became immune to the bites of the little devils.

I learned to milk cows by accident when I was eight. Mother had long wanted a cow and had finally got one, and we all watched with interest as she milked it the first few times, but then, quite unexpectedly, Mother got ill from a fish bone that penetrated the heel of her hand. The infection set in quickly, and aside from the fever and pain, there was a swelling so great that she was incapable of closing her fist and for ten days was unable to do anything about the cow. She was so weak that even had she been capable of milking with one hand, Father would have butchered the cow sooner than let her attempt it.

The creature had to be milked twice a day, morning and night, and the first evening Father talked the matter over with Mother, it was clear he had to attempt to empty the poor animal's udders before she became miserable. He was determindedly cheerful about it, not wanting her to worry, I suppose, but as he headed for the door he called "Come on along, youngsters," and I could tell that he wasn't looking forward to the experience and wanted us there for moral support.

"Will you get as much milk as Mama does?" asked Richard as we followed him up to the field, excited by the novelty of it.

"You'll be afloat in milk by the time I'm done," he answered. "Stands to reason, doesn't it, that if a woman can do it, a man could do it better." It was bravado, of course. Mother had forearms like a blacksmith when he married her, and although the muscles had wasted to some extent when she left off dairying for fishing, she was still stronger in the hands and arms than any normal man.

"I have a riddle for you, young bucko," said Father, and hastily added "and Keziah, you keep the answer to yourself," for I knew immediately what the riddle was going to be and already had my mouth open to tell:

Four stiff standers, four dilly danders
Two lookers, two crookers and a wig wag.

I helped as Father tied on the cow and laid down a handful of feed to quiet her, and she could sense that he was unsure of himself and kicked and moved about in a way we had never seen her do with Mother. Richard began gailing, because he'd figured out the riddle, which didn't help. Nevertheless, Father did his best, soothed the animal down and tried milking as Mother had told him.

After ten fruitless minutes, Father was shaking his aching wrists and threatening to make bully beef out of the cow. No matter what he did, he couldn't get so much as a squirt. After a time, the poor cow became almost as anxious as Father was to get the process going, but even after much to-ing and fro-ing from field to house and back, and lengthy simple instructions, there was not so much as a drop of milk. Usually only a restless cow needs to be stalled to be milked, and this one had always let down easily in the middle of the field, but we moved her to a makeshift stall in a shed, for Father had not yet built her winter quarters, hoping it would help. It didn't, and by then it was getting very dark indeed, and we were almost as agitated as the cow.

Mother thought perhaps it was the clothes that caused the problem, for it was well known among milkmaids that if you changed the colour of your dress the volume of milk dropped until they got used to the new one, but Father said there was no way he was putting Mother's smock over his trousers. It was Richard who said "Let Keziah try if the cow doesn't like men," so on went Mother's smock and back we went to the shed. I was a big girl and my mother was a small woman, but I still had to gather the skirt in a bunch at my waist as I made my way up the path. I made Richard stay behind as I knew he would tease.

"I don't think I can do this," I told Father as he sat me down on the stool.

"If you can't, then that's all there is for it, we'll have to ask among the neighbours. But Keziah, some things aren't learned, they are a natural talent and this may be one of yours. Look at those hands," he said as he held my palms upwards and began rubbing in the bag balm. "They look like they could empty the Milky Way."

I looked at my hands, which had always seemed so huge on the ends of my arms, and I remembered Father finding me with my hands in the chamber lye and saying "Enough!" and suddenly I knew this was what I had been waiting for, a chance to show him he'd done the right thing when everyone else said he was spoiling me. So I tried, and I can't say I did a very efficient job but I milked the cow that evening and again in the morning and then every evening and morning after that until Mother recovered from her injury. There was something so musical about the way the milk shot into the tin bucket, and the white, foaming look as it filled higher and higher gives the same satisfaction as a full berry bucket. It wasn't long before the cow started to let down her milk as soon as I started to wash her udders.

When Mother was able to take over the milking again, I was reluctant to stand aside—although I was relieved that she was better—but as often as not she had to go to the flakes or do some other chore. So I continued to milk the cow, particularly in the evenings when Mother was trying to use the last of the light to mend a few clothes or read one of the rare letters from home. Eventually, I took over the milking altogether, and I enjoyed it but in a way that was different than the way Mother did. My pleasure came from the tally of the pints and gallons, which to me represented money saved, and sometimes even money earned. Mother complained about how it took her from her chores on the wharf, but I believe she found milking the cow soothing, even restful, and in the early days I often heard her whispering and singing to the cow in the voice of her child-hood—she sounded like a girl when she spoke to the cow:

Come, come, cushy cow, come when I call,
Come, come, cushy cow, come to your stall,
Come, come, cushy cow, let down your milk,
And I will give you a gown of fine silk.

I knew the cow had no use for a gown, of silk or any other material, but when my mother sang that I believed the promise and was never surprised to see the milk come streaming down out of her hands into the bucket. However, my hands were large, as big as Father's even when I was a child, and the cow liked my hands more than Mother's songs, so I became the dairymaid. Mother probably missed the milking, and I certainly missed the songs, but the cow was as contented as any dumb creature can be and served us well until she grew old and dry and we sold her, on the hoof, to the captain of a French merchant ship who wanted meat for his voyage.

After I moved to Western Junction, I sometimes had as many as fifteen cows, but usually I had six, and I could milk those six in half the time it ever took any maid or man, including Kate who is better than most but who, for her sins, has hands the size of a normal woman. I've often had goats, and a goat is more interesting than a cow and easier to milk, but a goat can't be controlled and it will get into anything. I have merely tolerated chickens, for they are the smelliest creatures the dear Lord ever put on the earth, and troublesome even with their beaks trimmed and their wings clipped. As for pigs . . . it was a great relief to me when the train came and I was able to stick to cows and vegetables.

June 23

Hot and damp. Mumma seems a little better. I was telling her what I'd heard from Mr. Miller about the Hutton boys borrowing their sisters' clothes and performing a concert on the lawn when the professor arrived home unexpectedly, and I'm sure she laughed. Dermot has asked me to accompany him to an entertainment in Foxtrap this Saturday but I don't think it would be appropriate.

ate is working too hard, I can tell. Father Roche turned up just as she had finished putting the bread to rise, so she didn't even get a cup of tea before it was time to see to the linen. I could hear him in the kitchen, grilling her, although what it was about I couldn't say. His voice carries but you can't quite make out the words. Is that something they teach them in the seminary, I wonder? Very convenient for hearing confessions, no doubt. Poor Kate hates to be cornered and questioned that way—she always thinks she's done something wrong.

I heard the Big Galoot talking to her too, about going to a time up in Foxtrap, and she said she was too exhausted even to think about dancing. I know I discouraged her from going with him once before, and now I wish I hadn't for she needs to get out. She's slaving in the kitchen for the Knights of Columbus all day and sitting up with a dying old woman half the night. I used to worry that any match might turn out badly for my girls.

As it happened, Johanna was more interested in business than in men, and Min was so smitten with Jim that she wouldn't have listened if I had objected, which I never did because I knew it was hopeless. But I think I have done a disservice to Kate. I tried to keep her from becoming a slave to some man, and now she's a slave to me instead.

I never thought of myself as being in collar until I was twenty years old. From the age of eight, I had worked hard, but it was work I chose, and I was not taking orders from anyone. When my parents gave me direction, it was advice, and I was given liberty to ignore it though I rarely did for I well knew that blind obedience was what was normally expected from women and children, and that I was being given unusual leeway. It was in early June that Paddy first showed up at our house, late one evening, having walked out from St. John's after finishing his own work. It was warm for June, and I was airing out the house while Father was mending the roof, so the door was open with only a bit of sacking hung in the doorway to discourage the flies. I was in the kitchen, tying up the barm, when a headful of outrageously yellow hair poked its way through the brin.

"Now why would anyone be holed up indoors on a gorgeous evening like this?" said the yellow head, and I almost dropped the barm in my fright. I grabbed the broomstick right away, thinking it was a thieving sailor who had jumped ship in St. John's, and was just about to give him my opinion of his skull when Father came thumping down from the roof.

"You must be Mr. Aylward," said Father as he ducked in through the door. "The Bishop told me to expect a visit, but I didn't think it would be this soon." The Bishop? I didn't know what was going on, but this got my attention quick enough.

"At your service, Mr. Osborne, Miss Kezzy," said the yellow head, and made a mock bow first to Father and then to me. None but my parents and Richard ever called me Kezzy and right away I took a scunner against that ridiculous little

Irishman in the oversized coat, but it was clear Father was not unhappy to see the man. For one mad moment I thought that Father must have written to the Bishop in town and asked him to recommend a husband for me, but it was the Bishop who had written to Father, and out of respect for Mother he'd agreed to a meeting. I'd no idea he was so desperate to see me settled. Most of the young women in the Harbour were married and mothers by the time they were my age, for if the local boys didn't court them and secure them in the winter, one of the army of visiting summer fishermen would be sure to woo them and carry them off to St. Pierre or Lisbon or some exotic location where they would never be heard from again. Nobody had come courting me.

At mention of the Bishop, I immediately put aside the broom and listened. We had heard that his health was failing and that he had celebrated the first mass in the unfinished Cathedral on January 6th, the Epiphany of Our Lord, just in case he did not live long enough to do so at the dedication. The story Paddy told us that evening was more or less true—one of the men working on the Cathedral had been hurt when a harness had broken, and the engineer, who needed to inspect the roof, refused to go beyond the scaffolding unless someone was brought in to inspect and repair all the leatherwork. Paddy was at that time a journeyman cordwainer, and he was in the process of moving from one minor master to another—something he could afford to do, since he owned his own tools—so he was available to do a week of labour on behalf of the greater glory of God, and for his own greater glory, no doubt.

Paddy always had a good head for heights, and he was probably up and down the scaffolding far more than was necessary, putting on a show for the stonemasons and learning all about the pulleys that were used to move stone and men up and down the height of the building. When the harnessing was all over-hauled, he invited the engineer and the Bishop to come and inspect the results, but instead of just laying out the leather and canvas straps so they could be seen, he had the men rig up a bosun's chair. He demonstrated his faith in his own work by being hoisted fifty-five feet up at the facade, and then flown down the length of the structure, almost three hundred feet, to land with a thump next to the two startled but impressed inspectors. It's a wonder he wasn't killed, the foolish idiot.

I suppose that the Bishop, seeing a good Catholic Irishman with a solid trade and a willingness to work for the church, could be forgiven for thinking he was doing Father and me a great favour by sending us Paddy. The man was lively and companionable and hard working, though neither as sober nor as clean as I would have liked, but I mistakenly thought that could be remedied and I tried to put aside my misgivings. That hair of his always had the reek of rancid butter to it, a result of his running his hands through the curls after he'd been greasing up the boots he made. I couldn't abide the smell of it.

Father was taken with him from the very beginning. I've never understood that. Father was not one to be easily impressed, but Paddy's irrepressible energy may have reminded him a little of Mother, I suppose. Still, he was a first class journeyman, he was at least nominally a Catholic, and he was mad to have me when the rest of the world was indifferent. I made a lunch and served the two men, while Father beamed his approval and Paddy kept stealing sly glances at me and winking, and by the end of the evening it was evident that he and Father were of one mind. When Paddy finally left, Father turned and asked me what I thought of him.

"He certainly likes the sound of his own voice," I answered carefully, not wanting to give offence.

"Yes, he does, doesn't he," replied Father, delighted as could be. Clearly Father wanted this match to happen, and so did the Bishop or he wouldn't have sent this man out to us. I determined to please them both, and with luck to please myself as well. Paddy and I were married in the Oratory of the Presentation Convent by Father Troy on July 18th, the day after the Bishop was buried in the crypt of his unfinished Cathedral.

Paddy was ambitious, and marrying me improved his situation considerably, although I have to say he probably would have married me even if I'd had nothing as there were far fewer women than men on the island. I hated to leave Father, but he was anxious to see me settled, and that meant married, so I did my best to leave everything in order. Since I wasn't going to be around to look after them, we sold the gardens to the Angel family on shares, part cash and part product, and Paddy used the money to set up his first shop, a small rented place down on the bottom of Springdale Street that had narrowly escaped the ravages of the fire in '46. We had the front room, with a window and door on the street, and two rooms behind, with a small linney where the apprentice slept and where they stored overflow from the shop. He also had first one, and then two journeymen of his own, who did not live with us but who took their midday meal as part of their wages.

I had my first argument with Paddy over the apprentice. At that time, the shoemaking industry in the colony was very much in the control of the Irish, and Paddy's father had been able to arrange an apprenticeship for him from Ireland with a Kilkenny cordwainer who was moving out to Newfoundland. The papers were signed in Ireland, and were to hold for a full seven years, the terms including board and lodging, washing and a new suit of clothes. In return, Paddy had to keep his master's secrets, obey his commands, neither damage nor waste his master's goods, and was further forbidden to commit fornication, contract matrimony, play cards or dice, or frequent taverns or theatres. Paddy insisted his apprentice sign the same conditions.

I don't know how many theatres there were in Kilkenny, but there were few enough in St. John's and the apprentice, a nice little fellow of twelve, asked to be exempted from the condition regarding the theater because his older brother was involved in a revue being put on at the Garrison. Paddy, who never missed any of the traveling companies and who attended the Garrison theatricals with a dedication I wish he had displayed when it was time for mass on Sunday, refused permission. He said he'd been denied the theatre when he was twelve, and the boy must be denied it also. The apprentice didn't ask me to intervene but I did, or at least I attempted to, and it would have been better for both of us if I had not.

I gave the two of them a particularly good supper, and waited until the boy was in bed and Paddy was settled with his pipe in the kitchen. "That bedlamer is a nice little fellow, isn't he," I said, thinking to remind Paddy first of how fond he was of the boy.

"Good as gold and smart as paint," answered Paddy, or something to that effect.

"I noticed," I said, "that you gave him an extra helping of duff at dinner."

"A boy has to eat," he replied. "There's many a time I went to bed hungry back in Kilkenny." Now this probably wasn't true as his father was a respectable shopkeeper and would have placed him with a first-rate master, but I let it pass.

"So you don't think that just because you went hungry, he should go hungry?" I could tell from the look in his eye that Paddy knew exactly where I was headed, and he wasn't having any of it.

"Boiled duff is one thing, the theatre is something else. It would take his mind off his work," he said, puffing furiously on his pipe as if to add conviction to this nonsensical statement.

"But Paddy," I reminded him, "when you go to the theatre or to the tavern, you say it helps you concentrate better the next day."

"Don't contradict me, woman." By now his eyes were as red

and hot as the tobacco in his pipe. Paddy had the obstinacy of Balaam with his ass when he got his back up.

"I'm not contradicting you, you're contradicting yourself." I could tell I was headed in the wrong direction and tried to change course. "Now, Paddy, what's the harm in a bit of fun. You indulge the child in ways that most masters would find ridiculous, and yet . . ."

Well, I got no further than that, for he gave a roar, flung the pipe down against the stove where it broke into a dozen pieces, and after calling me a name or two that I heard many times in the years to follow, was out the door. He crawled in dead drunk long after midnight and struck the poor child the next day for not remembering to close the door softly. A week later he bought me a ridiculously expensive silk shawl and let the boy off work early to attend the dress-rehearsal at the Garrison, and when I tried to say thank you he behaved as if the whole thing had been a misunderstanding brought on by my nagging ways.

It's funny what will stay in your mind—we must have had a hundred arguments like that but this is the one I remember. The flanker from his pipe burned a hole the size of a walnut in the table runner my mother had embroidered—I can see the mend from here, over on the dresser, though Kate says I did it so carefully it's invisible to anyone else. That first spat was pretty well the model for all our disagreements over the years—they almost always ended in roars and name-calling and broken crockery, with a half-hearted attempt to mend fences a few days later. He never understood that a silk shawl didn't blot out the memory of the names he called me in the heat of battle.

I think I spent half my time that first year walking the road from St. John's to Petty Harbour, so worried was I by how my father was getting on without me. He had adjusted pretty well after my mother died, but then he had me to look after things so there was very little change in his immediate domestic arrangements. Without me and Mother, he needed help not only on the flakes but with cooking and washing, drawing water, sewing, all the small womanly skills that are not so easily acquired in old age. The day Father realized that I was about to become a mother myself, he forbade me to visit any more and quickly arranged for young Solomon Angel, who was promised in marriage to Margaret Lee, to move in with him. The two young ones walked back to town with me and were married that evening. Paddy got drunk as a lord at the wedding, and gave them both new boots which he'd promised to someone else for the following day.

It's hard to explain exactly what it was about Paddy that outraged me so. I suppose it was that he had so many God-given talents that he didn't use, or just plain abused. He was lively, quick, and the Lord alone knows women found him attractive, but he blew his own horn too much and too often, and he was never quite as good as he thought he was, for he cut corners and took on more than he could properly manage. Once, on a hot July day when he was working on a special order and didn't want to take the time to change into lighter clothing, he simply cut the sleeves off his best wool shirt with a clicker. He didn't even take the time to do it with a scissors, just hacked away at the cloth, and spent the rest of the week cursing himself for doing it, and me for not being able to mend what he had done.

When it came to bootmaking, however, Paddy had several advantages over the other small masters. As well as a natural dexterity that was a gift from God and no-one else, he had received first-rate training from his own master, who had refused to shorten the process from seven to five years as some did and who made him learn the business from the ground up. Then, he also owned his own tools, a gift from his father, which allowed him to move from one shop to another and learn all the secrets and tricks used to make a good business a better one. Lastly, he had a facility with languages that gave him an edge in buying leathers.

About a week after we were married, he took me with him to buy fine hides from a Spanish captain on board his vessel. I had always associated hides with the reek of the tanneries, but these hides must have been treated in some way for they were lovely-smelling coloured leathers, soft and supple, laid out all over the cabin. When Paddy opened his mouth and began to negotiate the prices, I thought he must be speaking Irish for I had no idea he could speak foreign languages, and it was many years before I could distinguish Spanish from French or Irish or Portuguese or German. Paddy spoke a smattering of all these languages, and when his knowledge of languages left off, his enthusiasm and determination picked up the slack. He could act out a part so that someone who was deaf, dumb and blind could understand him, and he did it in such an amusing fashion, that even if he couldn't offer the best prices, he always got the best stock available. More than once he made a few extra shillings by reselling a particularly fine bit of leather to one of the more fashionable bootmakers.

What stays with me about that first visit to the harbour is not the leather, but the food. Paddy had introduced me as his new bride, and after the deal was struck and the leathers bundled up to be carried back to the shop, the Spaniard insisted that we stay for a meal. The food was so unfamiliar that I cannot say I really enjoyed it, but I was amazed at the variety of both the taste and the look of it. My mother had been an excellent cook, and varied our diet as much as was humanly possible, I thought, but the basic elements were still biscuit, fish, salt beef or pork, and root vegetables, garnished with a few spices and very little else. Herring roe and melts, fried cod roe, a jar of pickled mussels, and now and again a creamed mustard or egg sauce were the occasional frills that made my mother known around the Harbour for her fancy cooking.

I've no idea what the Spaniard served me that day aboard his ship, but I decided then and there to find out a bit more about what people ate in town, and I think this set the groundwork for my eventual entry into the hotel business. Paddy, for all his languages, had rather pedestrian tastes, and the apprentices and journeymen didn't care what they ate so long as there was plain food and plenty of it, so I was somewhat restricted in scope, but there was still a lot of room for improvement. After a time I could serve the same four or five foods seven days in a row and never repeat myself once.

I can't take all the credit for making a success of the business, for I had my hands full with the household, but I did my best to be the "inseparable helpmeet" that I had vowed to be in the marriage service. In the house, I did all there was to be done, and I did it to as high a standard as was reasonable to hope for, and when my chores with the children were less pressing I did what I could to assist in the shop. I never made a shoe, nor ever cut or stitched one, for even if I had wanted to Paddy would not have allowed it. Paddy usually did all the clicking himself—matching the leather without wasting any was, he said, the key to a good boot at a competitive price. The closing, bottoming, lashing and sewing was done by the journeymen, assisted by the apprentice, and the polishing and finishing was done by the apprentice, assisted by me. I was taught to cut lace holes and insert eyelets, as well as to smooth down any irregularities, but even this was better done by a twelve-year-old boy than by me, for my hands were made for the plow, not the awl.

"As the Church is subject to Christ, so also let the wives be subject to their husbands in all things." Father Troy said this to us when we were married, but I have since read the service over many times and it also says in the service "Men ought to love their wives as their own bodies, for no man ever hated his own flesh." I tried to be subject to Paddy, but in some things it was not easy.

When I look into my heart, I confess that at the beginning I was hopeful, and even perhaps looking forward to the joys of married intimacy, for I could see that my mother and father were fond of one another and took some pleasure in even the casual contact of daily life. My mother, when cutting my father's hair, would lean into the curve of his back and massage his scalp before wielding the scissors, and when his feet were cracked and bleeding from being too long in wet boots, she would pull them into her lap in front of the stove and rub the cod oil into them as if she were kneading bread and often she would hold them in her hands long after it was necessary. Occasionally, on a warm summer evening, I would catch a look between the two of them and I learned not to ask questions if they disappeared for a time while engaged in some small chore down on the wharf.

I do not think I had unrealistic expectations. I had, even at the age of twenty, enough contact with animals, and yes, even some humans, to know that the joys of the marriage bed did not come right away for most of God's creatures. I was willing to be patient, but patience was not a word Paddy knew in any of the many languages he spoke. Sometimes he was rough or clumsy, and sometimes I wept, and this made him ashamed and angry. At first, he tried to soothe me, bringing me extravagant gifts we could not afford, or offering me elaborate compliments that no woman who owned a mirror could accept as sincere, when really all I wanted was a little more kindness and a great deal more time. After a while he stopped noticing my distress, or if I made him notice he told me I was a sullen bitch who refused to enjoy what any other woman in the town would be delighted to get.

I know to the day when I stopped hoping to enjoy my life as a wife and resigned myself to enduring it. Johanna and Min had been born, and a third pregnancy, another girl, had resulted in a stillbirth, so I was anxious and tense when I realized I was expecting yet again. It was too soon after my loss, and I had two small children to tend to, not to mention Paddy and the apprentices and the dinners for the journeymen. Yet I wanted this next child, wanted it very badly. All my life I had been blessed with good health, but this time nothing seemed to go right. I could not eat enough to nourish myself, let alone the infant, and day after day I bled a small amount until I could no longer be sure I was still carrying a child. The movement I felt was sporadic and weak.

I do not know how far along I was the night Paddy came home, drunk and disagreeable after a quarrel with his senior journeyman, for I had become pregnant so soon after the previous pregnancy that there had been no monthly mark for me to count from. All day I had been sick, throwing up what little food I could get down, and running back and forth to the earth-closet in the yard with the colley-wobbles. The children had been difficult and uneasy, infected by the unhappy apprentice who had to work between the two quarreling men, so I got everyone off early to bed.

I was lying, exhausted and sleepless on top of the blankets, when Paddy came into the dark room. He stank of the grog-shop and had no sooner kicked off his boots than he had his hands up my skirts and when I tried to push them away and whisper an objection, he clapped his hand over my mouth. It was all over in a few moments, and I don't think he even noticed the sopping rag I had between my legs to catch the blood that was again leaking out with frightening insistence.

I sent the apprentice for the midwife as soon as the first light broke, and while I gave birth, Paddy sat in the kitchen and vomited into a pail between his knees. The baby was bigger than I had expected, but small enough to give me little hope that she would survive. My father, when he saw her, said she had not enough flesh on her to bait a hook. There was a penny-sized wine-coloured stain on one side of her face that covered half her nose and part of her cheek, and when the midwife went to sprinkle the burnt flour on her cord to prevent infection, she jerked back and blessed herself for the baby had two extra tiny, pink teats below the regular ones. After that, I never let Paddy lay a finger on me except in strict compliance with my duty as a wife. I never made it easy for him to demand his conjugal right and I never pretended to like it. Like Pharaoh, I hardened my heart—I acquiesced, no more and no less.

I thought, given the circumstances, that the baby would die, and when she did not, I thought Paddy would reject her because she was neither a boy nor a pretty girl. I was wrong on both counts. Kate lived, and Paddy soon doted on her just as he doted on Johanna and Min. In time, she lost the unhuman look she had at birth, and as she grew the fading birthmark on her face did not. Even the extra teats shrank and soon looked like two little dimples that I told her were the result of bee stings suffered when she was left in her cradle on the stoop. But of my three daughters, I love Kate the most, for she cost me the love of my husband and my love for my husband, and she has grown up to be a woman of courage and compassion such as I never was nor ever could be.

June 28

Hot and uncomfortably humid. The Methodist Choral Society were returning to town on the train, and as they passed through all the young men pelted my cows with caplin. Dermot was furious, for we had to scramble to pick them up before the cows ate them and tainted the milk. We collected four and a half buckets full, and put them in the gurry pit. I told Mumma, and said it was easier than carrying them from Topsail Beach, and she blinked in agreement. Dermot is still angry—molasses pie for supper should sweeten him.

*L*izzie is here again today, I can smell her burning toast in the kitchen. School is over so I will see more of her now. Lizzie is such a trial at times, yet I long for the sight of her face as a shipwrecked man must long for the sight of a sail. I could hear her talking with Kate in the kitchen, and then there she was, with her solemn eyes and that tight mouth, peeping in around the door, looking for all the world like that photograph Mr. Tooton took of her out on the veranda last summer. I was awake for once, and I think I smiled because she beamed back at me. Sometimes I think I have said a word or two, or opened my eyes or mouth, but I haven't. This time I think I really smiled.

That picture of Lizzie is a treasure. He ambushed me in the kitchen, where I was plucking chickens with an old brin-sack around my waist, but Lizzie wasn't about to be caught out. She scrambled around getting her dress ironed, and then she had to have a little spray of fresh flowers for her hat, but it was worth it—so demure and proper she looked, perched on the corner of the chair with her ankles crossed just so. No frivolous smiles for Miss Lizzie Power, not for the camera at least.

There were smiles enough afterwards when I discovered that she'd got holes in her stockings and hidden them by painting her legs with India ink. Min was beside herself, but it was much better than having the picture ruined. Lizzie says there's a photo of Jimmy's grade one class on the wall at St. Bon's, and he's sitting in the front row with his leg stuck out so you can see two big holes in the soles of his shoes. Min's probably saying novenas every night, hoping the Virgin Mother will take pity on her and have some boy break the glass so they take it down.

Kate said Lizzie and I look more alike every day, but Lizzie said she couldn't see it. She wouldn't, of course. Why would a young girl of fourteen want to see herself in an old woman of eighty-odd years? But I have no doubt Kate is right, for I see myself in Lizzie and it probably goes both ways. I remember during Father's last going off, he looked younger and younger every day. So frail, he was, that he should have looked old beyond his years, but instead he looked more and more like a boy each day, more and more like Richard, with his hair stuck up in pooks and that rare smile dawning so slowly over his face whenever I was able to do something to make him a little more comfortable.

Paddy, for all his faults, was a great help to me then. He did for himself for almost a month while I took the girls to Petty Harbour, and he was out over the path every few days with any small bit of news to catch Father's interest or a treat he had found to tempt him to eat. If it was food, the girls usually got most of it, for Father was much better at not eating than I am, but to please Paddy he would try to take a small mouthful of the cake or fruit or whatever it was. Paddy once brought a whole hand of bananas, won on a bet with a Frenchman on a vessel sailing out of St. Martin's. They had the bunch tied in the rigging, to ripen I suppose, and Paddy went up the mast, dead drunk, to get his prize. It's a wonder he didn't fall and kill himself. Min was little then, she had never seen a banana, and she tried to eat it with the peel still on. Oh, the face she made, and now she can eat a banana every day of the week if she chooses.

Poor Father. All his plans—to move into town and live with us, to spend his old age with his granddaughters around his knee—all came to nothing. Ah well, he wouldn't have liked it in town, and his affection for Paddy would have worn a bit thin after a few weeks of having to put up with his bragging and his lying. It was just as well. But it hurt me to the heart to see him lying in that bed in the front room before his time, almost a corpse already. I didn't want him in there, for we hardly ever used that other room except for keeping things good and laying out the dead. Richard first, when the room was still almost new, then Mother, after that the Angel twins, because their family had nowhere to wake them, and then Father. Still, he insisted, and it was quieter there for him than in the kitchen, what with the girls up above in the loft. He never liked to make a fuss.

I recall the day he died, he had taken a little soup and then spit it up again, all over his shirt, so I washed him up and was pulling a clean shirt over his head when he turned his head as it came through the neck opening and he looked so like Richard that I couldn't help myself, but I began to cry. He gave me the sweetest smile, more like Mother than like himself, and said "You've been a good little maid, Keziah." And that was it. He fell asleep almost as soon as I laid him back in the bed and he never woke up. How I have consoled myself with those words all these years. I must try to say something for Kate before I go, but it is so hard, not knowing if the words are really coming out or if I am just imagining that I am speaking.

How Paddy carried on when he came that evening and found Father had died. You would think he was the one who had suffered a great loss, not me. He got the girls crying too, banging around the kitchen, pulling at that yellow hair of his and telling all our visitors that he had lost his best friend and the dearest man on earth. He was right about that, anyway. Father was a dear man. For all his gloomy predictions, he never stopped anyone else from having a good time. If Paddy couldn't dance, he didn't wish anyone else to, but Father wasn't like that. He took as much pleasure in watching Mother dance with the jannies as if he were dancing with her himself.

Not that Mother made a habit of dancing with mummers, only that last Christmas before Richard died. We never saw much of the jannies because we didn't keep strong drink in the house, but this one time they came and crowded in to the kitchen and the fiddler sat in the corner and played the Jew's harp while everyone sang. It was such a treat for Mother that Father lit the lamp, and Richard stood on a chair and sang "Eggs and Marrow Bones" and then someone arrived with a concertina. They moved the bits of furniture out into the snow, and Mother rolled up the mats and put them into the loft, and we had a real dance. I could see Mother's feet tapping and stepping while she clapped, and I never saw her look so young and pretty as she did that night.

When they called out that it was time to dance out the light, Mother looked so wistful that even Father had to notice, and when one of the jannies came forward and tried to pull her in with the dancers, Father gave her a little push too, and that was all she needed. I guess he figured one dance wouldn't be wrong, even if she was a married woman, but he hadn't counted on how solidly he'd built the house. At the last beat of the jig, all the jannies stamped as hard as they could, but our house was on such strong pilings that the floor hardly shook and the lamp barely gave a flicker. So they had another jig, and again tried to stamp out the light at the last note, and again the lamp kept burning.

The third time, I could see Father was getting worried about the stove, for he moved over to it and took the rag in his hand in case the chimney pipe came down. Mother was panting for breath and her hair was sticking to her forehead, but she was having a wonderful time, as light on her feet as if she danced every night of the year. Richard was hanging off the ladder to the loft, crowing like a little bantam cock, and when they played the last note, he shouted "Plank her out!" and every janny there stamped down as hard as he could on the floorboards and the whole house groaned like a cow in labour. I was near the lamp, and it gave me such a turn that without thinking I leaned over and blew on the flame just as it threatened to come to life again, which put an end to the dance. I was sorry, after, that I'd done it, but we'd probably had the best of the night by then anyway.

Afterwards, lying in the bed with Richard while Mother and Father put the kitchen back to normal, Richard told me that when he got older he was going to get a concertina himself and he would play for our mother so she could dance for him whenever she wanted to. Down below, we could hear the voices of our parents, so happy they sounded that it was like lying in a field on a warm spring day, with all the sounds of the insects and the birds and the cows in the distance, the whole world murmuring and talking with itself. We were never so happy before or since.

I watched Richard as he fell asleep that night, for the snow outside made the whole room light, and he lay on his back with his hair sticking up, and his mouth a little open, and I could smell the warm breath from his mouth, and I loved him that night like I loved my own children later. He looked so much himself, and yet so perfect that I couldn't imagine ever being angry with him for any reason. He looked just the same that day only a few months later when I leaned over the wharf and saw him in the water, his arms and legs spread wide, about six inches under the surface, except that then his eyes were open, looking up at me and not seeing me.

Death is such a mystery. How this weary old body of mine can hang on day after day, while Richard, who was so full of life and vigour and who still looked so perfect, could have been turned in a moment to a useless parcel of flesh and bone is something that I have spent a lifetime trying to understand. One rotten rung on a ladder, a tole pin left in a gunnel, a lump on his skull I could cover with my thumb, and it was all over. He never knew, probably thought as he tumbled backward off the wharf that he was going to get a soaking and perhaps a scolding from Mother. A soaking was a joke to Richard—he was like our old dog that way. Once, when Mr. Angel launched a new skiff, Richard followed it down the slipway right into the water, and Father's only comment was "There is nothing on earth that can excite a man like a new vessel."

Going into the water after Richard was one of the hardest things I've ever done, for the water was over my head and I had to hold onto the boat while I reached for him. I was unable to get out again until Father heard my cries and came to find us. I couldn't stop shaking after, even when Father had changed my clothes and put me by the stove with the mats over my shoulders. I've never been so cold in my life. Mother was in shock, I think, for she just went about dressing the body and doing what had to be done as if she were in a trance, but Father took the whole thing in immediately, understood right to his core that his only son was gone, and I could see him trying to control the wild grief in his eyes.

That night, Mama collapsed and he had to carry her to the bed and send to St. John's for a doctor to come in the morning. He got Mrs. Martin, the Protestant school mistress, to sit with me so that he could tend to her himself—he didn't trust anyone else, and all the Irish women were in the other room wailing over the beautiful boy, but he still found a moment to speak to me. He lifted me into his arms and held me tight, and then he said "Keziah, if I lost one hand I would still have another and I would cherish it all the more because I had only one. If I lost an eye, I would care doubly for the other."

"I tried to get him out," I wept into his ear. "He was too heavy."

"He'd hit his head and was already gone when you found him, I swear there was nothing you could do."

I wept all the harder, trying to believe him. "Nothing at all?"

"Keziah," he said, "what can't be cured must be endured. This thing cannot be undone. All we can do now is help one another endure as best we can. We must both look after your mother, for she is in very deep distress, but we must not forget to comfort one another as well. For the moment, she has forgotten that we need her too, but she will remember it eventually and she will come back to us again."

From that day I have regarded the sea with terror and disgust. On the sunniest morning it looks black and greasy; during a storm it foams at the mouth like a mad animal, and in winter it is a treacherous field of ice over a bottomless abyss. The greedy maw of the sea swallowed Richard in two minutes and then spit him out again to lie in God's small acre with Mrs. Cadigan's baby. He probably escaped a worse death, and I'm sure he escaped a worse life, for the sea was all he wanted and for most of the people in Petty Harbour, the sea provided nothing but poverty and misery.

5:00 pm

Dermot—

There is a loose board on the front step that has needed fixing for the past week. Do your job.

Miss Elizabeth Power

6:00 pm

Dear Miss Lizzie,

If a certain young snip spent more time in the kitchen helping her Aunt Kate who was up all night with Mrs. Donovan, and less time reading the trashy romance she has hidden behind the harmonium, I might be able to do my own work instead of hers.

Respectfully,
Mr. Derm. O'Dwyer

When I opened my eyes just now and saw the red reflection on the ceiling, I thought it was fire and my heart was halfway to the door before I realized that my body was going nowhere. It's only the sun setting and if the pounding of my heart would quiet down I will be able to tell the time from the noise in the kitchen below. It's such a warm day, Kate has put the shutter over the grill in the ceiling to keep the heat out of the room but I can still hear enough.

I don't suppose I'll ever lose my fear of fire—worse even
than the dread I have of the sea, although none of mine have
ever been burned, nor have we even lost a stick of furniture or
a bit of clothing if you don't count the boots Paddy burned
fighting the big fire just before he died. That was when the
stands of trees on the Southside Hills finally went, and haven't
grown back yet, it seems. Their roots were destroyed—the soil
was too thin to protect them. Paddy fought that fire with all the
other brigades, and then afterwards went wandering up through
the ruins of the hills where I used to get the spruce tips for the
beer, walking back and forth through the smoldering ruins of
the woods, until when he finally came home he'd burned the
shoe leather right off his boots and singed his feet so badly that
he could hardly hobble around for a week. He put the boots in
the window, nothing but uppers left to them, to show what a
big man he'd been, chasing around with the brigade.

I don't recall what started that fire. A Camphene lamp? A
candle left burning? It could have been any one of a hundred
things. It was a glue pot set off my fire, glue left on a stove in a
carpenter's shop on George Street, and a pipe dropped in a pile
of hay started Min's. I suppose every one of us is doomed to
trial by fire: "As the fire devoureth the stubble and the flame
consumeth the chaff, so their roots shall be as rottenness." It was
one of the reasons I hated living in town—the bells from the
Garrison going off every night or two and the acrid stink of the
smoke lingering and keeping you nervous for days after.

My fire had already started when I set out from the
Harbour to visit the nuns. I'd told Mother I was going to go
into town if I got the garden sorted out in time, and she went
on down to the flakes. When she saw the smoke from St. John's
rising like a pillar in the air, she walked halfway up the path and
saw I was still in the garden, so she went back to her work. I
wasn't there, though. I'd been restless, not able to settle down to
my work, and the crows were tormenting me, so I found some

old rags, bits of brin and old sacking, and tied them to sticks in the ground to keep those nasty birds off my new little plants. Then I collected a few pounds of butter, and I packed a dozen fresh eggs into a basket of moss, and added a piece of salt salmon, and started out the path to town. I was halfway there when I saw the smoke, so I took the road away from the river, heading more towards the Freshwater Valley, and turned down when I got past Flower Hill. I was so green—I just thought it was all an inconvenience, something I would have to work around.

Long's Hill was a good way from the fire, but it was still quite frightening to look down and see the flames whipping up in the wind, and when the vats of seal oil went up at Bennett's I very nearly gave up and ran home, for I thought it was the new gas works at Riverhead. That's when the wind changed. The smoke was blowing away from me then, so I went on to the convent thinking they'd need a bit of extra food for the people who were burned out. Even then I didn't realize how bad it was.

From the top of the hill, in the convent, you could hear the roar, like a gale of wind or a cataract, as the fire leapt from roof to roof, and then the crash as the roofs fell in. When the men from the Garrison blew up Stabb's house, the flankers exploded and reached as far as Circular Road and they even ignited the sails on the ships in the harbour. Two thousand houses were destroyed, they say. I heard after that an artilleryman was killed, and a prisoner they forgot about at the courthouse was burned to death in his cell. To this day I shudder to think of that poor man, trapped inside those stone walls with no way out. I don't think I have ever been so frightened, before or since.

At the convent, they were all business, clearing out the rooms to make pallets on the floor for the people who were homeless, finding clothing to cover the women and children who had lain abed too late and had to flee in their nightclothes. Bishop Fleming was still in England but Mother Mary ensured that everything was done as he would have directed it personally had he been there. I was hardly in through the door but the basket was taken from my hands and sent to the kitchen and I was put in charge of the youngest children, those who could walk but who were too small to help. A sad lot they were too— barefoot, runny noses and eyes, and covered with skin sores that a bit of soap and water would have soon cured. I got them into one corner, probably fourteen or fifteen of them, and began to make up stories, and when that ran out, I had them comb the tangles out of one another's hair and wipe their faces with a damp cloth until they all looked as respectable as they could manage. Mostly I was just keeping them occupied and out from under the feet of their mothers, who were wailing and tearing their hair at the loss of their few poor rags and chattels.

All this time, of course, Mother thought I was up in the garden, and every now and again she'd see one or other of the sacks I'd tied on the poles dance in the wind and she'd think it was my skirt or my pinafore. When I didn't come for my dinner, she was so annoyed she gave it to the new boy down at the wharf—he was so skinny, he'd eat an extra meal any time he could get his teeth on it. By mid afternoon the smoke from town was like a black cloud in the sky, and most people in the Harbour were packing up any blankets or clothing they could spare, for everyone had a few relatives or friends in St. John's. That was when she went to fetch me from the garden, and realized her mistake. Father was still out on the water, and she didn't even wait for him, set out instead on her own to find me.

Mother arrived just as evening was coming on, and I thank the Lord every day that she did, for I only knew enough to do as I was told and the good sisters were not as cautious as they should have been. The whole town, from Springdale Street to the Hill O'Chips was gone by this time, and confusion was the only order of the day. Collapsing walls were a great menace, and piles of looted household goods stood blocking all the roads.

Down at the harbour, the fire still raged, feeding on the oil soaked wood of the pilings, and the wind was so high that the engines could not get anywhere near it. Up at the convent, we felt relatively safe. Mother Mary stood in the doorway, giving orders and repeating to whoever would listen; "Jerusalem will have a wall of fire round about, and the Lord will be the glory in the midst of her."

I suppose we were all so overwhelmed by the noise of crying women and hungry babies, the reek of unwashed bodies and overflowing night-soil buckets, not to mention the permeating stench of the smoke from the fire, that one more smell escaped our attention. Not so Mother's. She was no sooner in the main room of the convent than she raised an alarm. At first Mother Mary thought she was hysterical, but soon I could smell it too—burning wool, like the Bishop's waistcoat a decade earlier. One of the poor refugees had brought a flanker rolled into a pile of bedding, and by the time we located the source, the entire back of the convent was on fire. We got everyone out, but the whole place was gone within an hour. The men who had been fighting the fires on the lower levels all day were too exhausted to drag their engines up to the top of Long's Hill, even if their horses hadn't been falling down in the shafts, and Bishop Fleming's beautiful convent was a pile of ashes and rubble long before daylight.

It was cold that night, much colder than one would have expected, and people huddled in the fields and streets wrapped in whatever rags they could find. The men from the Garrison set up military tents behind the Cathedral site, but there was no way room could be found for everyone in such a short time, and all the canvas was taken when we looked for shelter. We took refuge with the Mercy nuns, and in the morning we helped the sisters take what few things they had salvaged to the barn at Carpasia, the Bishop's farm. It was here that Father found us.

I will never forget that walk home the next morning. I was

sixteen, but I took my mother's hand on one side and my father's on the other, and kept my fingers well laced into theirs until we had escaped the town. We climbed up to Brown's field, and made our way down Military Road to the eastern limit of the fire, and then walked the length of the harbour, stepping over piles of charred wood and collapsed brick, skirting around hastily dumped barrels and boxes. Out in the Narrows, the customs officers were searching ships for looted goods and removing all unnecessary provisions in a desperate hope of feeding the inhabitants of the port through the winter. Dozens of small boats and large ships were lined up, bow to stern, waiting their turn to pass through and out of the razed city. Three times we were stopped by military patrols. All around us was a forest of chimneys.

In the ruins of one building, a group of men were pulling the bodies of two small boys out from under the remains of a chimney that had collapsed on them while they were searching for salvage. A woman, ashen grey and streaked with soot, stood dry-eyed and shocked nearby, clutching some unidentifiable metal objects in her apron. I don't know if she was their mother or their sister or what. Smoke still rose from the ruins of most buildings, and huge flakes of black soot hung in the air. Everyone, ourselves included, coughed and choked on the foul air. My throat was raw and Father could hardly speak, he coughed so much.

By the time we got to Kilbride Falls, it all seemed so remote and unreal that we could hardly believe what had happened. There was a small shrine set up near the falls, put there by the Walshes, I believe, before Bishop Mullock built the church, and we stopped there and washed ourselves as best we could. We drank draught after draught of the cold water, and Mother wet her fingers and combed the soot out of our hair as best she could, and then dried us off with her shawl. Sitting there on a bit of the bank, I finally lay my head in her lap and wept. I wept for the poor prisoner in the gaol, for the artilleryman, for the two little boys under the chimney, for the nuns who had lost their beautiful new convent, and for myself, for I could never again sleep without some awareness of the flanker in the blanket, the seed of fire ready to devour us in the night. It was not Thomas Salter or Paddy Aylward who took away my girlhood, but an ember brought into the house by a stranger I never knew.

June 30

Weather variable, changes every five minutes. Picnic book-
ings up for the weekend; have had to get Mrs. Walsh to
help. The girl was drying her wool stockings over the stove,
directly against my orders, and dropped one. The kitchen
was half filled with smoke before she realized what she had
done. Mumma knocked the jug of water off her dresser to
get her attention. I am in an agony over this—Mumma is
terrified of fire, and I know she would send the slovenly
child packing back to her family this minute, but I am short-
handed as it is, and the girl is hardly older than Lizzie. It is
my fault, for I didn't realize the poor thing had only one pair
of stockings and had been washing them out and wearing
them wet. She has only half a pair now. I cannot send her
home with even less than she had when she arrived, so I am
obliged to clothe her, whether she stays or goes.

*I*ve been examining my conscience and Kate is right, the
girl should be given a second chance. It isn't Annie's
fault she was dragged up rather than brought up to be useful
and clean. But I'd been thinking about the Great Fire, and it was
so vivid that when the smoke began to seep up through the
floorboards I was sure it was the end of everything. At least I
know now that I can move my arm if I have to. She doesn't look
like good material to work with—too sallow and drab—but
then I don't suppose I looked much like a farmer when I was her

age. If it hadn't been for the fire, I might never have thought to become a farmer for up until that time I'd never seen a farm.

I went back to St. John's many times in the weeks that followed the fire, to help the Presentation nuns who, refusing the offers of their sisters in the Mercy Convent, had determined to stay and continue teaching school at Carpasia. Like me, they knew little about farming, nor did the street urchins who were their especial charge, and they often required help getting chickens or pigs away from the outbuildings they were teaching in when the weather was bad. Often I would find them in the fields, beseiged by cows they were afraid to chase off, trying to quiz their little girls in their letters and sums while at the same time quaking in their habits from the benign gaze of old Bessie or Sir Grunt who merely wanted to chew the bit of grass they were sitting on.

Carpasia had only the minimum of staff, all the others having been ordered off to help in the town, so I was able to make myself useful, which is why Mother sent me back as often as she could excuse me from my duties. The Bishop had tried to sell the estate the previous year, planning to put the money into the Cathedral he was building I don't doubt, but fortunately there was no budding gentleman-farmer on hand to pay the price the beautiful gardens and the view could be expected to fetch. I for one was glad, for it was the first proper farm I had ever seen, a farm with a horse and plow, a harrow and roller, a manure pit and a boat for cods' heads. The coach house served as an office, for the coach had long before been sold to Dr. Carson, but to one side there was a small glassed-in shed for starting seedlings, and dozens of wonderful tools, even a gadget for crushing mussel shells to feed to the hens. I was happy to help reorganize the outbuildings if only to save these things from the prying, thieving fingers of the children who daily swarmed over the estate.

The Bishop came home two months later, and I'm told that he wept when he saw his city in ruins, and wept more when he saw the beautiful new convent in ashes, but wept most of all when he found his nuns sitting in the pig sties and manure pits of Carpasia trying to teach the little ones, and sleeping in the barn with the cows. They say this grief is what broke his health and led to his death, but I don't think so, for as always he turned and found practical solutions to many of the difficulties. Once again, I found myself at his side, taking his orders and implementing them with the assistance of a rag-tag army of corner boys and girls. We used hand-barrows and a dog-cart and quickly had things the way he wanted them so that he could go back to town with an easy conscience.

The four nuns, who had been sleeping in the barn, were quickly moved into the Bishop's cottage, where I knew he would have wanted them to be in the first place. I should not think ill of the holy women, but sometimes it seems that pride masks itself as humility. The cows were turned out of doors until a temporary shelter could be found for them, and the barn cleared out to make room for the children who came each day from the ruined town. The Bishop took two men off the work at the Cathedral and set them to erecting makeshift tables and benches in the barn, and they whitewashed the privy and built a barrier for modesty so that the children didn't have to empty their bowels in the fields where anyone might walk into it.

The men sent from the Cathedral were Italians, ship's carpenters who had been convicted on a charge of stabbing a third man on board a merchantman, and they were being allowed to serve out their sentence by using their skills for the greater glory of God. One of the nuns spoke Italian, having been to a convent in Italy when she was a girl, and she told us that these two were the devoted fathers of a large number of childen, and good Catholics as well. They adored the nuns and quickly turned their ingenuity to making the barn a cozy and comfortable schoolroom for the winter. Heat was not possible, for any fire in that building would have turned it into a death-trap, but they stacked the hay in such a way as to keep out the worst of the wind and snow and arranged small screens to keep the drafts down. There was a water barrel and a small shrine to Our Lady in one corner, where the children said their prayers in the morning, but oh, most glorious of all, they had painted the ceiling.

I don't know if it was their idea or the Bishop's but I remember walking into the barn with the sisters and the Bishop, to view the improvements, and when we looked up, there was a pale, blue summer sky with a golden sun in one peak of the hip-roof and a dark blue sky with a moon and stars in the other. I turned around and around, finding as I looked Cassiopeia and Aquarius, the Square of Pegasus and the Scorpion, the cross of Cygnus and the Pole Star, all my old friends. The Bishop laid his hands on my shoulders and turned and turned with me, until we were like two dizzy tops, and we laughed and laughed until we fell down into the straw, but the nuns simply stood there and cried. I have never understood nuns and to this day I am puzzled by those tears.

MRS. KEZIAH ALYWARD

1880

PATRICK DONOVAN

1880

MARY & THOMAS POWER

1898

JAMES & ELIZABETH POWER

1908

Elizabeth Power

c. 1910

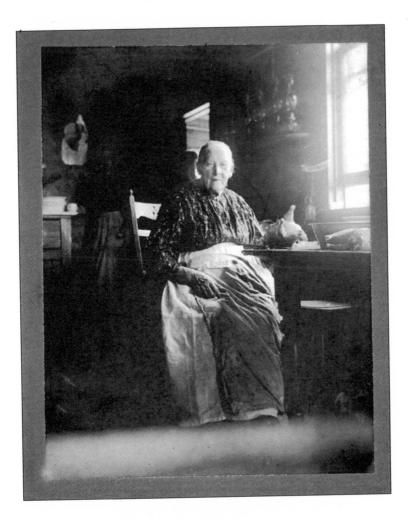

KEZIAH DONOVAN

c. 1910

KATE AYLWARD O'DWYER, PROPRIETRESS
DONOVAN'S STATION C. 1915

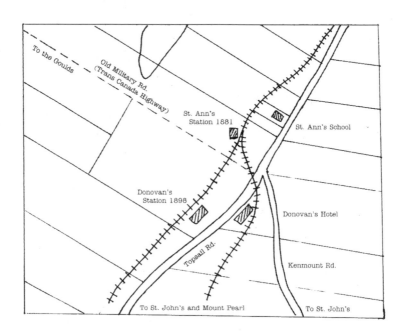

WESTERN JUNCTION

July 1

Rather doubtful looking, rain. Fr. Roche stopped on his way to town—just had the train stop ten minutes while he looked in at the door at Mumma. Said he'd be back on the weekend. What does he want with us?

*L*izzie is full of surprises today. This is the third Sunday in a row she has come to coax me to eat. This time she appeared with a bowl into which she had put a mashed potato, a dipper of gravy, and a quantity of finely chopped chicken oysters. Some of the ladies who come for tea this afternoon are going to be disappointed when they start digging among the bones. I managed only a mouthful of it, but it was very good.

"Nan, do you remember the time out at Littledale you brought me the chicken?" She sat there with the spoon in her hand, looking very serious. How could I forget? Mrs. Walsh from down the line had been over at the convent visiting her niece who was about to take final vows, and she stopped here with a message from Lizzie: "Tell Nan they don't give us enough to eat and I'm hungry." Mrs. Walsh said she thought Lizzie looked as plump as a partridge in a berry patch and it was all stuff and nonsense, but my heart just ached, thinking about my little girl going to bed with pains in her stomach, and first thing the next morning I set out, walked all the way, for she was only five and when you are five a day can seem terribly long.

I had a whole chicken cooked and wrapped in a bit of oilcloth, hidden away in my basket under the ginger bread for the nuns, and they said it was breaking the rules to let the girls have visitors during the week, but since she was the youngest there, and no doubt they wanted the gingerbread for their own dinner, they let me take her out into the garden. She climbed up a tree with the chicken and ate the whole thing, dropping the bones down into my skirt where I was resting my aching feet. I swore I'd never forgive Min for sending her away, and her hardly more than a baby, but I suppose with the stepbrothers and Min newly widowed, it couldn't be helped.

"Nan, I wasn't really hungry. They gave us plenty to eat, but it didn't taste nice like your food and I was angry at Mam and I wanted to see you." Lizzie was staring at the wall when she said this, like it was a great sin she was confessing. I tried to smile but it must have looked like something else for poor Lizzie looked very guilty and dismayed. "Oh, Nan, I'm sorry now, I didn't stop to think what a long way it was, and I didn't know you would have to walk. Mam had sent me out a pair of boots, ugly rubber boots, and I hated them so much that I wouldn't wear them, but then a few weeks later I got my feet very wet and the sisters said I had to wear them or I wouldn't be allowed out. I was longing to be with the other girls and when I went to put the boots on I found she'd filled them with Jerusalems, all done up in beautiful coloured wrappers. There was one for every girl in the school, and three left over that the nuns said I could have all for myself."

Poor Min. I'd told her Lizzie would rather have one beautifully wrapped candy than a hundred common mints, or even a dozen Gibraltars, but I didn't think she'd listened to me. She is at heart a shopkeeper, and she'd rather sell her best and eat the rejects. Lord knows there were plenty of rejects when she first started the shop. Even the boys got tired of powdery bulls-eyes and scorched peppermint drops. I couldn't for the life of me figure out what she was doing with all those cabbages I was sending out to her, and all the time she was using the leaves for wrapping the sweets until she could afford to buy waxed paper. I never thought she'd make a living selling oranges and apples, not at those prices, but the confectionary business is like the liquor trade—always a market no matter how poor people are.

Lizzie's confession about Littledale was only her first surprise, but the second one I anticipated for I smelled it coming up through the grill. Min had purchased two hundredweight of green coffee and sent some out on the train with Lizzie. I could hear the big frying pan banging on the damper as she roasted the beans, and then the smell of the oil went right through the house. After Lizzie gave up on the chicken, she brought me a cup of coffee, hot and thick with cream, and I did a bit better with that, though I think I got the best of it in anticipation.

Her third surprise wasn't so pleasant, but I think I hid my feelings for Lizzie didn't seem to notice. It was a letter from Johanna to Min and Kate, saying she wasn't able to come and visit—no surprise there, for the hotel business is no different in Boston than in Newfoundland. She has offered to take Lizzie next summer, and will pay for a tutor so that Lizzie can try for entrance to the Sacred Heart College in New York. My little Lizzie at school with all the well-to-do young ladies . . . I'm not so sure I like that idea as much as I ought. I don't think the Sacred Heart Ladies will be as impressed by the Central Fruit Store as the girls of Littledale were. Still, Johanna has neither chick nor child of her own and it's about time she did something for her sister's daughter. Lizzie wants to go, that's certain. I can't say I blame her—she can't spend the rest of her life pulling toffee on the candy hooks, and with no father and no inheritance except the little I have put by for her, she will have to look after herself. I'm glad she has taken her letter off to show Mrs. Walsh so I can think about this without her watching me all the time.

It was funny, Lizzie being so angry at her mother about the

boots and harbouring that resentment even when she was five. We have a great talent for holding a grudge, me and Lizzie. I was upset at Min for getting a husband who already had two boys, and then upset at him for dying and leaving her with two more children, yet I liked those Power boys well enough, better than Min did, I think. She was a good stepmother to them, gave them an education and saw they had the best she could afford, even better than her own two, but she never really warmed to them, I thought, no more than she warmed to Mr. Donovan. I swear she held a grudge against young Thomas simply because he had his father's name so she couldn't give it to her own boy and was forced to name him James Thomas Power instead of Thomas James Power.

I like to think I'm slow to anger, which is perhaps why it takes so long for it to dissolve once it finally appears. Paddy had such a capacity for infuriating me when no-one else could, and he seemed to take a particular delight in provoking me to any open display of temper. He didn't succeed often, but even once was too often for my liking. I always felt so defeated when he got me to raise my voice or even start banging the pots in the kitchen. It's curious, but Mr. Donovan always laughed when he detected irritation in me, and it sweetened me somehow. Min's Tom was the same way—whenever she was giving him a piece of her mind, he'd stick his tongue in his cheek and roll his eyes like one of the wharf rats caught with his hand in the apple barrel, and instead of it making her worse, it made her ease up on him. He was so comical.

Min always said that Tom was like Paddy, but I never saw it myself. Of course, she was only a girl when her father died, so she wouldn't have remembered the nights he came late to supper, three sheets to the wind with a couple of Spaniards or Frenchmen in his wake, or the times he misled the customers, blaming the late boots or the bad leather on the tannery when really he had sold off the material to a higher bidder. Tom was never like that—if he made an error, he admitted it and he never allowed a servant to take the blame for something he had done or left undone. He liked his drop, and I feared he was going the way of Paddy at one point, but he had some excuse, being twice widowed before he was even thirty, and with two motherless boys to think about.

Once, when I had gone into town to see Min, after Lizzie was born, I saw him in the street, his coat awry and his hat looking the worse for wear, as he was himself, and I was so ashamed for Min that I turned into Ayre's and pretended to be looking at the dried fruit in the bins so as not to have to meet him. He saw me, though, and saw that I had avoided him, and a week later he travelled out to the farm to tell me that such a thing would never happen again. I thought he would be angry at me, but he was only angry at himself and he promised that I would have no reason ever again to wish he wasn't my son-in-law. When he left, he kissed me as if I had been his own mother and the day he died I wept as bitterly as if he had been my son.

Min needed someone like Tom in her life—she was always far too serious, always trying to keep up with Johanna, which was impossible. When Tom died, I thought she would bring the children back to live with me, and help Kate in the dairy, but instead she got old Andrew Delgado to help set up her little shop selling fruit and confectionaries. Johanna was always a favourite of Mr. Delgado, and he did it for her sake, I expect. Min's shop is a far cry from the Delgado's. They brought that beautiful curved glass all the way from Portugal, they say. Going in there is like a trip to Lisbon or Paris—the Malaga grapes and the figs and dates and whole hands of bananas, all the exotic fruits and the colourful novelties, the painted fans and silk flags.

Min makes a living, and she gives good change. She may add a coating to the cocoanut bars when they get a little lumpy, something to fancy them up and cover the unevenness, but that's what any good cook will do, for even the best cooks make mistakes. The ingredients are pure and wholesome, which is more than can be said for some of those fancy British confectioners. Her oranges are Delgado's rejects, but she has nowhere near the markup that old Mr. Andrew has, and Mr. Andrew, however fond he is of our Johanna, is not exactly a model of probity. When his first wife died, her sister ran all the way to Torbay to tell their mother that Margaret was finally rid of that old demon. Her mother thought that Margaret had murdered him, and was heartbroken when she realized it was Margaret who had died, not Andrew.

I've been surprised by Min more than once in the years since she grew up. Johanna was always bold, Kate was always shy, but Min veered first one way and then the other, and I thought that with Tom gone she'd lose her grit, give in entirely to the black dog that always seemed to sniff at her heels. She was born with a morbid streak, like Father, and looked around for misery when experience tells us that it will find us soon enough anyway.

How I used to laugh when they played Dead Baby on Saturdays. I gave those girls a dozen washings of arms and legs during the week, and wiped their faces a hundred times a day, it seemed, but Saturdays they always had a proper bath, and clean shimmies and night-dresses. When they finished their baths, they looked like little angels, all starched and white with their hair brushed out to their waists. Min used to coax the other two to lie down with her on the bed with their white nighties pulled as smooth as could be, and pretend they were all killed by the cholera and ready to be photographed. They'd manage to stay still for all of a minute, perhaps.

After Johanna got tired of being dead, the two of them would pick on poor Kate, who would do anything to please them. They'd lay her out on my little sewing table, with a shawl draped over it, and put flowers they'd fashioned out of paper and scraps of cloth around her head and feet, and a tiny Bible in her hands. Min would be the mother and Johanna the father, and they'd cry real tears. Little Kate would be bored stiff and more than once fell asleep before they'd finished mourning her properly.

Dead Baby gave one of the neighbours a horrible turn once, for she stepped in to ask to borrow my big jam skillet one Saturday evening and thought it was the real thing. Thank goodness it wasn't Mrs. Smyth who saw them. It seems odd now that it didn't bother me, seeing them laid out like that. Perhaps it was because it just seemed like they were going to sleep. Real death was the Cadigan baby, stinking and covered in sores.

I remember once I went with Father into the woods to cut some knees he'd marked, and on the way back we saw a caribou, just one all by itself. Father had his gun, as always, but by the time he'd put in the powder and all, the deer had moved some distance away, so the shot didn't kill it, only wounded the poor creature in the gut. The two of us ran after it, and it kept stopping to look back at us, as if it wanted us to catch up, which eventually we did, and killed it of course. Father was all out of breath and trying to get his knife out, and he called to me, "Hold its head, Kezzy, talk to it a minute," and I did. I stood in front and wrapped my arms around its antlers and I could feel the warm nose through my coat, and I don't know what I said but it seemed to work for it didn't try to break away.

Poor creature, its eyes were huge. Then Father felt with his fingers and pushed the blade of his knife down behind its head to sever the spinal cord, and it gave a shudder, just the way Egypt shuddered with pleasure when Richard came into sight, and then it was still. Such a strange feeling I had at that moment—I expected to feel disgusted to see the beautiful creature lying dead on the frosty ground but instead I was half ecstatic at what we'd just done. Helping to kill that deer seemed one of the most beautiful things I'd ever done in my life.

Paunching and butchering the carcass was a dirty job, for the ball had punctured the stomach and it was quite a mess to work with. Father cut it all up in jig time, and wrapped it in the skin, and we left the head with the spruce knees to fetch later, but the foxes had picked it clean by the next morning. Father made me a mat hook out of the antler once it had dried, as well as three coat hooks for Mother and a crook-knife handle for Richard. I still have the mat hook in the bottom of my old Labrador box. The first mat I ever made of my own design had a caribou on it and I was so proud of it, I had Mother turn it face-side down except on Sundays. When it finally got so worn it was good for nothing but the men's muddy boots, I burned it in the stove rather than see it ruined.

Another call from Father Roche, Kate says. I can't think what he wants with us—perhaps it is because I was Bishop Fleming's pet, and Ned Roche will do anything to be seen as his successor. I don't know why he is out in Topsail anyway. Hiding his tuberculosis from Archbishop Howley, perhaps. He'd never make the Terna if that was known. Or perhaps he's just courting the likes of R.J. Murphy and the wealthy Protestants. He puts himself forward too much—I don't care for that in a man, not even in a celibate. It's the quiet, steady ones who have always gained my respect, men like Mr. Donovan.

The evening I first took notice of Mr. Donovan was like any other. I had decided to break up a small bit of meadow and plant flowers for the market in St. John's, just to try it out, and had arranged for two men who had been working on the railway line to give me a week of work when they were finished. I agreed to pay them the usual wage, and to give them their meals, and in addition I told them they could sleep in the barn on condition that they did not smoke except out of doors. I understood that both were discharged naval men, so I knew if they said they would not light their pipes, there was a good chance they would not, for most former military men have learned the hard way to obey orders given for good reason, or even for no reason at all.

They worked well for me, or so Kate said for I did not have the time to oversee what they were at, so I was not discomfited when I heard someone stamping and scraping his boots outside the kitchen door that evening as I finished kneading down the bread. I have no idea where Kate was—usually she was with me in the kitchen, but this Saturday night I was alone—but I was neither young nor frail, nor helpless either, and a visit from a transient labourer was no threat to me. I hardly bothered to look up when he entered the kitchen, but finished wrapping my bread pan in a layer of old quilts before putting it to rise behind the stove.

"I've a deadeye, Missus," he said, and held his hand out to me, palm up, as simple and plain as a child.

"And what is that to me?" I asked, not in an unmannerly way, for I had no reason to feel hostile. I was merely curious.

"I will be little use to you on Monday if I do not do something for it now, and old Scrappy Jack can barely piss straight without someone telling him to, so if you want your field ready before the snow falls, you will need me to see to it. And I cannot fix a deadeye on my left hand, since I am contrary." It took me a moment to realize he meant that he favoured his left hand rather than his right.

"Sit," I said, and tapped the table to indicate where he was to settle. A good worker needs looking after, just as a good horse does, and I had no reason to think this man was not earning my dollar honestly. He came forward and waited with a stillness and patience that I well appreciated as I rooted around in the barrel chair in the corner for a bit of wool and a needle. "Let me see the gall," I said, once I had found what I needed, and he turned his hand, palm upward, on the table. In the middle of the palm was a hardened blister the size of a shilling. Settling into a chair, I laid out my instruments—a hank of wool, a needle, a jar of hardened pork fat, and my smallest scissors. I lifted his hand into mine, and was suddenly, awkwardly aware that my own hand was as large and as callused as this young labourer's.

"It's been a trouble all summer," he said. "Mostly I ignore it, but the gall just gets bigger each time." He was not complaining, just telling me. I took the bit of wool and dipped my fingers in the fat before I began to twist it into yarn. He said nothing more and I said nothing more. For a full minute I tried to thread the yarn into the needle, but my close-vision had recently begun to fail me and even with the stiffened yarn I was clumsy.

"Let me," he said, and taking the needle and yarn from me he quickly threaded them.

"Are you certain you trust me to do this?" I asked, and I was surprised to hear a slightly unsure note in my own voice.

"I have been eating your cooking for three days now, and you haven't poisoned me yet," he replied with a laugh. "In fact, I can hardly remember the last time I ate so plainly and so well."

"I cook plain because that's what the men want," I replied quickly, even more astonished at the hurt note in my own voice than I was at his praise. Most men notice what you give them to eat, but don't think to comment if it is good, only complain when it is not.

"I trust your hands even if I don't trust your eyes," he answered, and once more placed his hand in mine. I took the threaded needle and quickly pierced the gall, drawing the greased yarn through so that the two sides were opened, and then I quickly snipped off the ends so that there was about an inch of yarn left in the palm of his hand. I bedded the gall in a bit of raw wool and bound it with a strip of linen.

"Done," I said, laying the scissors down on the table, and trying to look as if I was sure of myself.

"And well done, I'd say," he responded, and laughed. "Has

your eyesight gone recently?" he asked. "My sisters all lost their close-vision when they stopped having babies." I didn't know where to look. A common labourer, in my own kitchen, saying such things to me. He must have noticed how I stiffened, for he immediately pushed back his chair and stood. "Forgive me if I have been too familiar," he said, not meeting my eye, which would have undone me altogether. "I was a great deal with women in my early life and I forget sometimes that there are things that are not remarked upon outside the family." And before I knew it he was out the door.

I did not see Mr. Donovan the next day, for I went over to Topsail to attend mass, and stayed the night there visiting with the priest's housekeeper, Mrs. Coady, but on Monday evening when I got back, he stopped me as I was going to look at a cow that had been sick.

"I am looking for a place for the winter, Mrs. Aylward. I was wondering if you could help me," he said, as he held the barn door open so I could pass through.

"We don't keep anyone over the winter, Mr. Donovan, I'm sorry," I answered.

"I'm not looking for a berth," he said, most politely. "I am going to speak to Mr. Smyth about using the tilt in the back wood-lot on his property, in exchange for working on his fences. But I understand from Mr. Walsh that you are going into St. John's tomorrow to get your winter provisions, and I thought perhaps I might go in the long-cart with you. If the matter is settled, I could carry back some things I will need."

I thought about his request as I examined the cow, which did not seem particularly unhappy, having consumed a half gallon of blackstrap molasses that morning, according to Kate. The man was civil and there seemed no reason to refuse him.

"I'd be glad for the company, Mr. Donovan," I said, "particularly if you will give me a hand loading up my own things. I find the storehouse boys at Ayre's are sometimes careless in the way they stow the barrels and I'd rather not lose my flour on the road." I paused for a moment and then drew a breath and risked being thought a gossip. "A word about Mr. Smyth—he's a capable, honest man, but he often leaves his memory in the bottom of a glass, so when you speak to him on business, address your remarks to him but make sure Mrs. Smyth is at hand. She is the real brains behind that operation. That way, whatever terms he agrees to, you can count on them remaining the same."

"I appreciate your advice, and I should like to offer some in return. I am told that you can buy spectacles for a very reasonable sum at McMurdo's. Unless, of course, you are one of those women who prefers to look well than to see well."

The man was as brazen as a robber's horse. "Do I look like that sort of woman?" I asked, shaking my apron, which as usual was covered over with an old flour sack to keep the dirt of the barn off my kitchen clothes.

"No, you do not, which is why I make the suggestion." He told me later that I was as indignant as a wet hen, which may or may not have been the case, but he certainly looked highly amused at my reaction.

In any case, we set out the next day, and I was careful that the sacking and the apron were on the back of the kitchen door, and my hair and dress were tidy and clean, and by the time we got to the Military Parade I had forgotten all about his boldness and had found him a pleasant and thoughtful companion. As we drove into the town, I began to think about the extra items Johanna had asked for, and took out a slip of paper on which she had written her list.

"Well, Mr. Hawkeyes, can you read this for a blind, old woman," I said, mocking us both and waving the paper under his nose.

"No, Missus, I cannot," he answered with a smile. "You will have to make McMurdo's your first stop."

"Enough of your nonsense," I laughed, "just tell me what's

on the list and I will think about McMurdo's before we head home."

"Really, I cannot read it for you. I can manage a little print, but I never learned cursive at all, and I am totally unable to write so much as my name." He did not seem bothered to make the admission, but I confess I was much surprised, for he seemed a sharp enough man, and exceptionally well spoken even if he was a labourer.

"It's the result of being sinister," he added, holding up his left hand, healed now from the deadeye. "I went to school to a brutal little hunchback, down in Broad Cove, and the master would put the chalk in my right hand, and before you know it I would suddenly feel his belt across my back and discover to my great astonishment that the chalk was inexplicably in my left hand again. He told me it was a great sin I was committing, but I felt no guilt, and didn't even know I was doing it." He smiled wryly as he rubbed the slight scar in his palm. "After two weeks there wasn't a patch the size of a penny on my hands and legs where he had not applied the strap, and despite his tender ministrations the chalk still made its amazing leap from my right to my left hand, so I gave it up. I accepted the beatings but I got tired of standing with a ten-pound Bible over my head all day. My older sisters taught me the alphabet, but I have never been able to piece together more than a dozen words on paper, and those only the most common ones." He imparted this news almost cheerfully.

"I took a good many of the best from Miss Lacey down in Petty Harbour," I told him, "and I could read and write better than she could when I arrived in her school. I just found it easy, I suppose. She married an old widower more than twice her age and my former schoolmates tell me he paid her back for her temper many times over."

Mr. Donovan laughed. "And Mr. Belbin got his reward, as well. He had a tame pig that followed him everywhere, broke into the gardens and tipped over the gurry buckets and nobody dared stop it. One winter day it got into his mash bucket and, drunk as a lord, it attacked the man, took a piece out of his backside the size of his hump. He could never sit down comfortably again and spent the rest of his miserable life on his feet."

Then Mr. Donovan took the reins out of my hand. "I'll mind the horse while you speak to Mr. McMurdo, or Miss Johanna will have to do without her few things until winter."

So I went in and got a pair of spectacles in a tiny hard case, and when I came out there was Mr. Donovan waiting and I climbed up in the cart next to him.

"So, what is it that Miss Johanna wants?" he asked. He was trying not to smile, and I was trying not to blush.

"I'll go over her list later, after I go to Ayre's," I answered, busying myself with my basket which suddenly needed close attention.

"I thought you weren't that kind of a woman," he said, and this time the big grin was unstoppable.

"Oh, very well, you win," I replied, and took out the little black case and the list. Once the spectacles were fitted on my nose, I looked him straight in the eyes, but of course he was suddenly very blurry for the glasses were only good for close up.

"Very handsome," he said. "Very dignified." And to my astonishment there wasn't a hint of mockery in his tone. "And now I shall leave you to do your shopping and when you are finished your business and I am finished mine, you will find me at Mr. Foran's store eating his excellent ice cream, after which we will load your provisions and, with luck, my own as well."

And that is how Mr. Donovan came into my life, as pleasantly and as quietly as a sunrise in summer, though of course it took several more months before I realized what was happening. Min had ructions when she saw what was coming about, and said I was making a fool of myself with an ignorant young lout who wanted nothing more than an easy berth. Even the harsh words from Johanna did not distress me as she hoped, for I knew by then that he was the kindest and gentlest man in the world and that he loved me even though I was ten years older than him and could bear him no sons or even daughters.

It is such a mystery that I found it easy to love Mr. Donovan without trying at all, and couldn't really love Paddy although I tried with all my might. You cannot know who you are going to love or why. I have attempted to keep this in mind when I see the Big Galoot making cow-eyes at Kate. I have tried to tell her that she is free to make her own choice regardless of what I or anyone else thinks, but she is not as stubborn as me and he does not have extra courage to give her such as Mr. Donovan gave to me.

July 6

Clouds, but pleasant. Mr. Conroy came for supper, with his wife and several of the older children. I was not expecting them but managed a fine platter of trout, and cheese rarebit for the young ones. Mr. Conroy seemed somewhat uneasy and asked me in private what I thought my mother's chances were of recovering her speech. He then requested permission to show any of Mumma's papers related to Bishop Fleming to a representative of the Archbishop (Father Roche?) and implied that there was some talk of Beatification. Mumma never kept letters and things, burned them as soon as they were answered, and I told him so. Dermot, who I happened to mention it to, said Roche would sooner see Mumma's Bishop frying in hell than Beatified. What a shocking tongue that man has. I told him what I thought of him. Fr. Roche is a priest!

Mr. Reid has sent out four bottles of Hunt's Port, to stimulate my appetite. It was very kind of him, but I expect it will do about as much good as the pan of sea water Mrs. Coady put under the bed to stop the bed sores. The paralysis is fading but I am so weak that I am as good as paralyzed anyway. Still, I can utter a few words in recognizable form, which is a useful skill though not one I choose to exercise very often any more.

When Kate brought the glass of port with a spoon, I was

able to give her a smile and waggle my finger at her to drink it herself. She did too, which surprised me. She sat on the side of the bed and stared at the ceiling, much as I do myself these days, and said nothing but just drank the wine like a good girl. I suppose she has a great deal on her mind now, what with the hotel to worry about and the Big Galoot to nail down, if that's the route she decides to take.

Kate was always a good girl. I thought she was too good to live, at first, for she didn't even cry when the midwife baptized her. Oh, I was so angry at Paddy. I decided that I would keep the midwife for the full ten days, even though it cost him two pairs of his best boots, and I did nothing but lie nursing the poor scrap of a baby while the midwife fended off Johanna and Min, and gave Paddy a feed of tongues whenever he dared to complain or talk back at her. On the up-sitting day, I decided we were both going to live after all, and when the midwife suggested I come down to the kitchen I pulled myself together and got into my proper clothes.

She had tea laid out on the table, with the groaning cake which was just a bit of raisin bread, and five cups. There was me and the midwife and the two little girls, who were barely able to see over the edge of their cups, and then Judith, who was living in behind us at that time. Paddy never used her name, just called her "the barrel woman" as if that was all there was to her. I'd seen her now and again, coming and going to work or helping Mrs. White get the clothes in when the soot from Newman's was coming down and marring the clean washing, but we'd never spoken. It was the midwife who brought her in—said I needed a guest to eat the groaning cake.

Judith was a fine woman, for all her rough ways. I'd never had a friend before, never needed one perhaps. After the midwife went her way, Judith would stop now and again to empty the night soil for me, for I was weak as a newborn myself, after Kate. She knew Paddy didn't like her stopping in and always slipped out the back way when she heard his footsteps coming through from the shop. A few months later, when I thought I might be that way again, I told her and had a little cry and she brought me a bit of tansy, made it into a tea, and watched while I drank down all the bitter stuff. I'd seen women with the tansy tucked into their bonnets, to keep the flies off, but I didn't know 'til Judith told me that it was good for women's complaints. I tried it once more a year or so later, walked down by Rennie's Mill where I knew there were plenty of golden buttons, and it brought on the flow and after that I never got into that condition again before Paddy died. Towards the end I wouldn't let him put a finger on me anyway, I was that angry.

I look back now and it is hard to know why I got so enraged. Accidents happen—even the most vigilant mother must take her eyes off a child now and again. It happened to me once with Min. The door didn't latch behind me when I came in from the yard, and she slipped out and was gone for at least half an hour before I even missed her. I was frantic, sent the men from the shop out into the rain to search for her, imagining her dead under the wharves or kidnapped by a Spaniard who was even then sailing out the harbour. They found her in an alleyway, up by St. Patrick's, with a rainspout from a building tucked inside the neck of her dress at the back. The downpour was sluicing over her, and she was sitting in the middle of a pool of water, enjoying herself tremendously. To this day she claims she loves the feel of summer rain on her face.

Yet it seemed to me that Paddy had been particularly remiss, though I know in my heart that he loved the girls. It was a holiday, not St. Patrick's Day but some day later in the spring, and I was cutting a dress for Johanna. Even at that age she must have a fitted dress, not a chemise like her sisters, and Paddy offered to help me stitch it. He always gave in to the girls, wanted to see them dressed like little ladies, and since he could sew a fine seam—better than I could, if truth be told—he would help me and coax me into adding deckers and lace enough for any princess.

Paddy had a message to do over in Maggoty Cove, so he took the two small ones with him and left me in the kitchen with Johanna in her shift, trying to give a waist and hips to a child who had none yet. It was a nice holiday for all of us. There had been a fine sprinkling of snow and Kate was wearing her first proper clothes, and a leghorn straw hat with pink roses and ribbons on it that Paddy had bought for her. She and Min looked so sweet and ladylike, going down the street in their best boots, trying to put two of their footprints in each one of Paddy's footsteps that had melted the snow on the road. Their little legs could hardly manage and he shortened his stride, so he was like a duck with its young ones tagging behind.

I don't know how long they were gone, but I had the dress cut and Johanna had gone off to visit a friend over in the lane, when Paddy came back with Kate wrapped in his jacket and tucked under his arm, and Min hauled along on his coattails. Kate was soaked, blue with the cold and shivering. They had met up with a man Paddy used to work for, and the two men had been talking while the man's little boy took the two girls down to the Lower Battery. The children had scampered down the cliff path to the water and climbed into a small boat moored there, pretending to sail around the harbour. The boy used an oar for the push off, and when the boat jerked to a stop at the end of the mooring line, Kate, who was standing in the stern, fell into the water. Min, God bless her, reached out and grabbed her by the hair and held on while the boy went screeching up the path to get the men.

I took Kate and stripped off her clothes, and sent Paddy out back for a bit of blasty bough to get a hot fire going. It was all very frightening though not really anyone's fault, but then I found the hat squashed into Paddy's coat, bleeding pink all over the straw. Kate, who was looking better every moment, grabbed out for the hat and pulled it under the quilt with her. Min told me that even after the men had pulled Kate from the water, Kate had howled and fought until Paddy got in the boat and fetched the hat out from under the stage.

Paddy was back in the kitchen then, and I'd got the hat back from Kate and was trying to straighten it out, when he bragged—yes, he bragged—that it had taken him ten minutes to get the hat out from under the wharf, but gotten it he had. Ten minutes! The child was sitting on the stagehead, wet and cold with snow on the ground, and Paddy had gone fishing for a hat! "Papa won his wager," piped up Min, and then clapped her hand over her mouth. At that moment, Kate had leaned forward and snatched the hat from my hand, and put the wet, bedraggled thing on her head with a triumphant "Katie's hat!" and that's when I went mad. I grabbed the hat from her head and hit her across the face with it, the pink dye and the ribbons leaving a slash mark on her cheek as if I had whipped her with a belt.

I've never been so sorry about anything in my life. Johanna was standing in the doorway, and Paddy and Min were at the table, and they all saw me hit the dear baby—poor, frail Kate with her blue skin and her wet hair hanging around her pinched little face. And it was all Paddy's fault. He was the one I should have hit, but by the time I realized that, it was done, and he was across the room and gave me the back of his hand so that I went over a chair and hit the stove with my head. The children were all crying, and Paddy was hanging onto Kate and Min and Johanna all at once, and I'd have gone for the carving knife except that I couldn't have got at him through the children.

It was never put to right between me and Paddy after that. I apologized, and he apologized, and the children all apologized, and the hat went into the stove after Paddy promised Kate another just like it, and in half an hour we were all sitting down to our dinners, but I never forgave him. He thought I never forgave him for the blow he gave me, but it wasn't that—it was the blow I gave Kate I couldn't forget. I confessed it to the priest that night, up in the Cathedral, and he said that he didn't need to give me absolution for striking my own child, especially since I had been provoked by fright and righteous anger, but I made him assign a penance and I made him give me absolution, for if ever I sinned in my life it was that day. All else I did in the months that followed was nothing compared to it.

I was never Paddy's wife again after that, and I didn't care if he got the priest to me or not. I hardened my heart against him. I washed his clothes and cooked his meals, I helped in the shop and I worked harder than I had ever worked before or since to see that he had a well-run household. I took over the book-keeping for the shop, which had always been a trial to him though he was clever enough with numbers, and we had our best year ever. I scoured the doorstep so that it was white, and I polished the stove so that it was black, and I used whitewash to paint the special notices on the window when Paddy was trying something new. I coaxed the apprentices and flattered the journeymen and curtsied to the customers, and everyone said what a wonderful match Paddy Aylward had made, and what a lucky man he was to have a woman who was such a hard worker and a good manager.

But one thing I did not do was let him touch me as my husband again, never again after that. At first he let it go, thinking I'd come round, and then he got angry and tried to bully me, and he even threatened to call in the priest, but I was unmoved. It said in the wedding service, "Let not the author of deceit work any of his evil deeds in her . . . let her shun all unlawful contact." Being with Paddy had led me into sins of thought, word and deed, for I would have driven the kitchen knife right into his heart that day if the children had not surrounded him, and I was never going to let him bring me to that point again. As long as my body was my own, I could tolerate anything, and

I think he must have known it for he found a clicker under our mattress one day, an old one I had sharpened up and put there for him to find, and after that he sulked and cursed and went to the trollops in the lanes but he never forced me again.

Two years later he was dead and buried and I had made my escape to Western Junction. It's a pity I never told Judith about the clicker. She would have liked that part.

July 9

Hot day. Rained last night but burned off early. Mumma tried to get out of bed in the middle of the afternoon and fell. Dermot was mending the front step and heard her so he ran up and found her on the floor. After he lifted her back into bed—no easy feat as I know myself—she struck him. He says she is old and sick and frightened. She is frightened of no one and nothing, not of God Almighty Himself. Why does he let her treat him that way?

The cat got into the house and when Lizzie crawled under my bed to get her out, she tipped over the pan of salt water and soaked her dress. Lizzie has a mind like a steel trap—argued that there was no rational reason why a basin of sea water should stop bed sores, which are caused by chafing, as if it was Kate's fault the basin was there. Mrs. Coady must be a trial to Father Roche, with all her superstitions and her old-fashioned ways. I'd just ignore it but the Reverend Father seems to think it is the thin edge of the wedge and we will all revert to idol worship if he doesn't stamp out such practices. She casts spells right under his nose and he doesn't recognize it.

Oh, that's a dreadful thing to think about a good Christian woman, but she really is fearfully superstitious, and it's not really fitting for a priest's housekeeper. Lizzie says it's shocking ignorance. Judith was like that. Good, kind Judith. I wonder what ever happened to her? Sometimes my memory is so unreliable, like the screen door in the kitchen after Jimmy poked it full of holes with a pencil. When I worried inordinately about something, Mr. Donovan used to say "'Tis nothing, 'tis a hole in the ground," but you can fall into a hole and hurt yourself. Judith was older than me, so she'd be close to a hundred if she were alive today.

The day we became friends was the day the *Ida* was launched. Little Kate was only just deciding to live, and Paddy closed the shop and took Min and Johanna and the two apprentices over to Mr. Kearney's shipyard to watch them bring the new ship through the archway and across the street to the harbour. No doubt he had a wager on it—half the men in town did. I must have heard Paddy tell the story a hundred times of how Mr. Kearney was so sure that Mr. Bennett was wrong when he said the ship would scrape her sides, he was willing to risk his gold watch, which he hung on a nail driven into the brickwork. The *Ida* cleared the watch by two inches and came down into the water without a mark on her.

If Paddy had been in the house, Judith and I would never have become friends, but there was nobody home except me and the baby, and Mr. MacDermot out in the shop, finishing up a small job of work. I knew that he was leaving us at the end of the week. There was no future for a Scotch in St. John's, not in the shoemaking business anyway. He was too good to work for Paddy—Paddy liked good work but hated good men.

There was Judith, calling into the open door as she went by to see if I needed anything. Such a quiet, warm day, I was finally feeling better than I had in months. The bread was put to rise and the baby was asleep, and the kettle just on the boil, so I asked her to stop for a minute and I noted that she was limping as she came in the door. She laughed when I asked if she'd hurt herself. "You'd think it's the hands that would go first," she said, and held out her hands, palms upward. They were all cracked and callused, and the fingers were crooked like claws. I'd seen worse down by the flakes in Petty Harbour, but I looked at my own hands, soft from bathing the baby and putting up the dough, and I wished I could do something to say thank you for all the times she'd stopped and emptied the night soil bucket because Paddy forgot.

"I suppose if I had to wear boots on my hands, and walk on them, they'd hurt just as much as my feet do," said Judith, and settled with a groan onto the settle next to the baby. That's when I thought of the jar of lanolin I had from Father, and in a trice I had her boots and stockings off and her feet soaking in a pan of hot water. I put a fresh kettle to boil for tea and took the boots out front to Mr. MacDermot. He was a big, quiet man and I'd had little to do with him, but I'd always made sure he had an extra potato with his dinner and I counted on him having noticed.

There was nothing wrong with the boots, he said, but he came back into the kitchen and had a good look at Judith's feet, taking them in his big hands and feeling the bones, and then he said he'd need the boots for half an hour. Judith was uncomfortable at the attention, but she was there with her feet in the pan of water and there wasn't much she could do about it. I made tea and brought a pannikin of it to Mr. MacDermot, and two slices of bread and jam, and then Judith and I had our tea. I could hear the racket of the crowd at the launching and I knew there would be a cheer as she went into the water, so we had plenty of warning before Paddy and the others would be back.

I took a plug of Paddy's tobacco, and shaved a little of it into the basin of water, for Mother had said that an infusion of tobacco was good for rheumatic bones and I hoped it might help Judith's feet. "Mrs. Aylward, I think I've died and gone to heaven," she said, dabbling her feet in the water and blowing on her tea. When Judith smiled, which wasn't often, it was a smile that could light up the room. All the misery and depression I'd felt while I was sick with Kate just seemed to blow out the window, and I thought how easy it was to make someone happy.

I asked her to call me Keziah, because she made me feel like an old woman, calling me Mrs. Aylward, and I said if she was married she'd know how old and tired that can make you feel. I don't know why I just assumed she had never married—perhaps it was because everyone called her by her first name. Most of the barrow women were married, and those that weren't were widowed, with a dozen children to feed, which is why they chose to do such hard work. The wages weren't as good as the men's, of course, but they were better paid than most women doing unskilled labour.

"Oh, I have a husband, Mrs. Aylward—Keziah—and you're right about marriage making you feel old and tired." She nodded at the baby, who was asleep next to her. "Not that I was ever blessed or cursed with one of those little darlings. When I hear women complaining about their children, I just say 'All my children are perfect' and when they figure out what I mean, they give me this pitying look." I tried not to give her that same look myself. Even on the worst days, my girls made life with Paddy tolerable.

"And where is your husband, Judith?" I asked, being too stupid to know that if things were all right between them I wouldn't need to inquire.

"Today, he's probably digging potatoes. I visit him on Sundays, out on the farm."

"And what farm is that?" I asked, not thinking what I was stepping into. I often dreamed about having a farm of my own, and took any opportunity to find out more about the ones in the district.

"Oh, it's a very special farm, Keziah, I expect you've heard of it. Palk's Farm." And then she saw the look on my face, and laughed. "Oh, I shouldn't tease you, please don't take offense. Yes, he's in the lunatic asylum, God help him, been there for years." She reached over and patted my arm, sorry for having played a joke on me. "He's happy enough, poor soul, and he's the star inmate so they don't torture him or mistreat him. Besides, I keep a close eye on what goes on, and if there was so much as a mark on him I'd have them all before the magistrate."

"And is he really a lunatic, Judith?" The cheerful way she talked about him seemed to invite questions.

"Crazy as a March hare," she answered. "He could leave any time he wanted, but he has found his place there, and they won't make him leave because he is so good with the other patients. He all but runs the farm, and there are some really violent inmates that no-one but him can go near, so they keep him on as a pauper, and I bring him new clothes when he needs them, and a bit of extra food, though usually I come home with more than I've brought as he's really the best farmer on the island. I sometimes think that George has worked out the perfect arrangement—hard work and reasonable food, in exchange for never having to make a decision or worry about anything except getting your eye plucked out by a fellow inmate." She laughed again.

That day was the only time Judith ever talked about George. He had what she called an excess of rum and religion, if by religion you meant a strong belief in ghosts, phantom ships, witches and such things. She said he'd made a study of the Book of Meditations, a foul volume—the lurid details of the damned in hell would give any imaginative soul the horrors.

George, according to Judith, had once been a fisherman, with a side-business in smuggling loaf sugar, liquor and tobacco from St. Pierre, and he got into trouble when a tidewaiter was overzealous in the performance of his duties. The tidewaiter had come to his house and tried to arrest him one night, and George had refused to submit, had instead stuffed him into the woodbox and threatened to kill him. Judith was there in the house with them, and she said this was the first time she realized just how deranged he had become from reading the Bible and sampling his own contraband once too often. She reminded George that to kill the tidewaiter would be murder, a mortal sin, and he argued that surely it was only a venial sin considering the man's profession. After a few more tots of rum and considerable reflection, he decided that a tidewaiter wasn't worth the risk even of purgatory, so he let the man go and then fell asleep by the fire. They took him into custody the next morning.

Judith followed him into town, when they brought him to trial, and he lasted two days in the prison before he tried to cut his throat, but he was rescued in time and his throat was sewed up. "That was just like George," Judith said, as she patted the baby who was stirring in her sleep. "He never could get anything right." After prison, it was the lunatic asylum, and that's where he stayed all the time I knew Judith, or at least I assume so because every Sunday I saw her walking west on Water Street with her bundle in her hand, and sometimes she'd bring me back fresh vegetables or a carved wooden toy for the baby.

In later years I visited the farm at the lunatic asylum but I never saw anyone that fitted Judith's description of George, and they knew of no long-term inmate called by that name. Perhaps she made him up for some reason. Whatever the truth of it was, Judith was the saving of me, for though we saw little of one another, she was the only person I ever spoke to about Paddy. She had taken a violent dislike to him without ever having spoken to him, and while she couldn't do enough for me or the children, she would go so far as to pray that Paddy would choke when he coughed. She said nothing when the girls were around, thank goodness, for I couldn't have let her in the house if she had tried to turn them against their father, but when we were alone, she vented a spite that was shocking and unbounded.

Once when I was feeling particularly distressed over some misdeed of Paddy's—one of his usual lies or infidelities—she put a curse on him that she claimed bounced back at her, for that day she slipped on the wharf and almost broke her elbow. She stopped by to let me put a compress on it and when I wasn't looking, she slipped a pissing bottle in the stove to cancel the curse. A few minutes after she left, I heard something crack in the coals and as I lifted the damper the smell of urine was unmistakable. When I cleaned the grate the next day, there was a lump of glass fused to the clinkers. In the months that followed, when we were together in the kitchen and we could hear Paddy's voice from the shop, yelling at one of the apprentices or joking with a customer, I would see her rub her elbow and mutter under her breath.

Paddy returned her dislike, with just as little reason, but unlike Judith he made no bones about it to the girls. He called her a witch, and claimed he could smell sulfur when she had been in the kitchen, and said he'd be only too happy to put the torch to her. I don't suppose he would really have burned her as a witch, but would possibly have given her a good scorching as a warning. Once Min asked her if she was a witch like her dada said, and Judith just smiled and said "Of course I am, my darling," as if she had asked if Judith were a Catholic. I have to admit now that Judith was perhaps a bit crazy herself.

That day, though, I saw none of that side of Judith, all I saw was a hardworking, tired barrow woman with sore feet. Just as the cheer went up to signal that the *Ida* had gone through the arch safely and was well on her way to the water, Mr. MacDermot came back into the kitchen with Judith's boots. He warned her that they would feel a bit uncomfortable for the first few days, but that she should persevere and before the week was out her feet would feel like those of a girl of ten. By the time his prediction came true, he had left for Nova Scotia, but Judith begged a bit of his old apron off me and made up a charm to keep him safe and make him wealthy. I heard years later that he eventually owned a factory with upward of a hundred employees, up in New Brunswick, so perhaps her witchcraft worked. I prefer to believe that a man who could in twenty minutes make a shoe insert to cure a bad foot had earned all the success that came to him.

July 12

Fine, sunny day again. Mumma has apologized to Dermot, said she was confused. He looked embarrassed for her. No visit from the itinerant clergyman this week, thank goodness. That man makes me nervous, not like dear Father Walsh. I find myself writing the most surprising things in this small diary—I had better tuck it out of the way in case Lizzie or the girl happen upon it. It took me five years to fill the first half and now it looks as if I will need a new one before the summer is out. It's just as well—it keeps me from saying things that I might regret. Inundated with Orangemen, all surprisingly well behaved, considering, but then it is Sunday.

Kate looked tired this morning. I think it is the extra work, looking after me, and I wish she'd get Mrs. Coady to help, but she says it's only that a mouse was gnawing at the picture railing in her room all night. That must be why the cat came in. After the lightning hit in 1907, I chinched up the hole over the railing with a mix of flour and salt, not having any lime and thinking the salt would make it unpalatable to mice, but that was seven years ago and perhaps the salt has leeched out. I should tell her to remove the salt-dough and plug the hole with lime or a bit of steel wool.

Funny, the way the lightning hit. I can see the shadow of a black smudge on the wallpaper here in this room where it passed through. I'll wager Father Roche said more than his prayers that night. We got off easy—there were boats on the collar turned bottom up in Blackhead, and a horse struck on Thorburn Road. And of course that poor woman in town, on Colonial Street, burnt to a crisp in front of her husband's eyes when the kerosene lamp went up. She must have taken a direct hit. They say she was cooked like a rabbit—they couldn't even move the body without a shovel for the flesh fell away from the bones and the bones from one another.

I don't recall ever seeing lightning like that before or since. There was once when I was a girl, but that was in the middle of the afternoon. Winny Weir—the one we always called Wormy Weir—thought the gunboats were shelling the harbour. I expect her family came here before the anti-settlement laws were revoked, and she'd been raised with the fear of being burned out by our own navy. It was exciting, the lightning. Mr. Donovan was gone to Harbour Grace to see about a new cow, and I wondered if he could see the lightning from there. It was so dark, even with all the lamps lit in the house for the supper, and then every once in a while there'd be a flash and the crash following it. I could hear the men in the dining room, counting together and laying bets on how many miles away it was.

Mr. Reid was acting as croupier that night—who was the dinner for? Someone from the *Calypso*, the paymaster, I think, not someone from here. There was Mr. Alderdice, and Mr. Outerbridge, and half a dozen Harveys. I know Mr. Greive was with them, for he brought me a case of aerated water for the Church Lad's picnic the following week. When the lightning hit, every lamp in the house went out and we took the thunder in the dark. What a racket went up then.

There were only thirteen for dinner because one of the party was a doctor who had been called away to a patient, and they asked me if there was another guest who could join them, to dissipate the evil omen attached to thirteen at the table. I told them Father Roche was upstairs in the side bedroom, the room

Kate's in now, but I doubted he'd co-operate though I didn't say so. Mr. Reid went and spoke to him, and came away a little annoyed, I could tell. I suppose Father Roche was only following his conscience, and he probably knew by then that he was about to be raised up to vicar-general and didn't want to do anything that could be talked about, but I have never thought it would do any harm to accommodate a bit of frivolous superstition.

So I told them that I had two of Mr. Perlin's Russian peddlers in the back linney, nice clean boys though they didn't speak a word of English, this being their first time going with their packs around the bay, and they went and coaxed the two out to sit with them. I made sure they got a nice bit of chicken instead of the pork pie and ham the others were eating, and they sat like two little crows, watching the gentlemen enjoy themselves. I expect those two have their own shops on Water Street by now and will be gentlemen themselves before long. I was just bringing in the duff, and a beautiful egg custard with cream and bottled bakeapples I had put up myself, when the streak of electricity came in along the telephone wire and the whole house lifted up its skirts and settled back again with a bang.

The entire place was pitch black, except for a bit of flame coming off a glass of brandy that was sitting on the mantlepiece. I could hear the maids screaming in the kitchen, and the two peddler boys saying their prayers, and then Mr. Reid saying in a calm, low voice "Did I hear a pin drop?" and the whole room went up in a shout of laughter. My hands were shaking so much I could hardly light the lamp, but somehow I had managed to hold onto the tray with the desserts, for it would have been a real mess if I had dropped that, and not another bite of sweet in the house except some fruit cake and a barrel of biscuits from Woods, which would have been a poor finish to a very good dinner.

What with getting the oil lamps lit and dealing with the two girls with the vapours in the kitchen, I almost forgot about Father Roche. We had examined the damage downstairs—the lightning tore the moulding right off the wall and flung my engraving of "The Death of Nelson" across the room before it went out to the verandah and splintered two pillars—and the men were just sitting back down at the table when I heard the priest calling out for a light. Well, I ran up the stairs as quick as I could, given my size and age, and he was sitting in his chair next to the window with his breviary in his lap. I lit the oil lamp and we looked around the room, and there was the mirror on the floor, still intact, and the splintered frame on the wall.

"You'll be Pope before you're done," I said, thinking of his good luck and his ambition and forgetting for the moment that he would never admit to having either, and he frowned at me, but I could see he was very thoughtful and even a bit shaken by the whole thing.

"I'll have none of that superstitious nonsense attached to my name," he said, and then told me I wasn't to mention the incident downstairs. But I saw it in the paper the next morning, not in *The Telegram* but in *The Herald*, so he must have told someone himself for I mentioned it to no-one, mostly because of what I found when I went to my own room. The dinner was a great success, notwithstanding the lightning, but I suppose the lightning strike made the men more excitable than usual and they stayed on playing cards and drinking until close to two in the morning. By the time I saw the last of them off I was the only one left awake in the house, Kate having walked Ettie Walsh home and stayed the night with her to calm her down.

I could hear the two little Jews snoring in the back, and the future Pope sawing wood up above them, and the peace of God descended on the house like a prayer. Then I went into my own room and right in the middle of our bed, mine and Mr. Donovan's, was a little tintype I had of the two of us, taken a year or two after we were married, and one side of it was blackened and burnt while the other was untouched. It was Mr. Donovan who was blackened out and I knew it was a token. I took the picture and bent it inward into two and then folded it again and pressed it flat under the heel of my shoe, and then I crept down to the kitchen and put the thing in the stove, poked it with a stick into a good bed of coals, and went back up to bed to wait for dawn, for I knew Mr. Donovan would be home as soon as ever he could make it.

He was first off the train next morning, as cheerful and healthy as a man could be. He told me that a Harbour Grace woman by the name of Yetman had her house split in two by the lightning and her dog, which was chained onto the house, was killed. The cow he'd gone to look at was older than had been claimed and the stable wasn't clean so he'd decided against buying her. We looked at the two verandah posts, which were chopped into splinters as cleanly as if it had been done with a knife, and traced the zig-zag mark on the coping back into the house, though the dining room and up into the bedrooms. I showed him "The Death of Nelson," or what was left of it, and the mirror, and we looked at the hole along the telephone wire. He left me to deal with the minor damage and set out to repair the verandah before any more guests arrived. I never told him about the tintype, and he didn't notice it was gone.

There was a lot of talk and head-shaking over at the railway station about the dinner of the previous night, and speculation as to what might have happened if the two peddlers had not been at the table. I didn't join in. I wished then I had the certainty of Father Roche that omens are nothing, not even the devil's work. But I didn't forget, and I watched my dearest husband with a keen and worried eye and was there to catch his head that day six weeks later when Father Roche was appointed to the Cathedral and my Mr. Donovan put his spoon down in the middle of his dinner and died in my arms.

I had a lot more sympathy for Min after I lost my own husband. I tried not to make such a fuss as she did, for it wasn't seemly in a woman my age to go around grieving so much in public, but it was hard. Later that winter I fell coming in from the barn with the milk, and broke my hip, and it never healed, but in some ways it was a good thing to have happened. Before, I would sit in the kitchen trying to peel potatoes or pluck partridges, and as soon as my mind was free to think as it wanted to, I would feel this terrible pain, and I'd wonder where it came from. Afterwards, I could locate the pain in my hip, and sometimes it was so great it stopped all thought.

At first, after Mr. Donovan died, I tried to take on all the work of the farm and the hotel that he had done, but I wasn't as young as I had been so at Kate's bidding I hired the Big Galoot. He has never been half as good as Mr. Donovan, but he did fix me up with a special chair so that I could work in the kitchen without too much discomfort, and Kate seems to feel confident with him. It's she who will be giving the orders around here soon, so that's important.

There was a lot more for Kate to do once I was stuck in the chair, but I tried never to complain and I did almost as much sitting down as I had once done standing up. It gave Kate complete control of the barn and much of the house, which was good for her. I have been too large in her life, too quick to take responsibility off her shoulders, so she has never developed the resilience she needs to make it through life on her own. I will say nothing about the cat, but will let her solve the problem of the mouse on her own. It is past time she was allowed to suffer the consequences of living in this vale of tears without her mother trying to soften the blows that inevitably fall on those of us who have hearts.

July 23

*Fine, sunny day. Mumma slept all morning and all after-
noon, or pretended to. Ate nothing. Quiet day, only one
gentleman for dinner, none for supper. Worked on the
accounts. I looked in on Mumma as I was going to bed, and
she was awake. I offered to say the rosary with her, and she
gave a little shake of her head and whispered "Not tonight."
Instead she had me go into her Labrador box and take out
several things she wished to give to Lizzie. Hidden away at
the very bottom was the mat hook she so treasured, and I
asked if she'd like to put it with the other things, but she
managed to tell me that she didn't think Lizzie would be
making many mats after school in Boston. She asked if I
would like to have it, and I got very tearful for I know her
father made it for her when she was a child. She also gave me
a small holy card with a quotation on it that she had used to
mark her Bible, and said that when she died, I was to do
whatever felt right to me and not to listen to Min or anyone
else. She was quite drained by the effort and after taking a
spoonful of milk to wet her lips, she closed her eyes again,
but I suspect she is too exhausted to sleep. I have the feeling
that she spent the whole day summoning up the strength to
speak those few sentences to me.*

I have given my last scrap of advice to Kate—from now on, she will be making all the decisions herself. When Paddy died, everyone kept telling me not to make too many decisions right away, everyone except Sister Mary Magdalen O'Shaughnessy. While the men were at the funeral, the good sister came to sit with me and she gave me a gilt-edged card with a sentence written upon it: "The only way to begin a thing is to begin it immediately." This was one of the mottoes of Nano Nagel, the Holy Foundress. Little Kate was near my knee at the time, and as I read the words, she ran her forefinger under the letters. Looking down at her pinched, white face, made paler and more fragile by the black clothing she had on, I determined to get her and her sisters out of mourning as soon as possible and into a healthier, happier life. I took those words to heart and made up my mind at that moment to sell the shop as soon as possible and to look for a property outside of town, away from the filth and stench and noise of St. John's.

It was Sister Mary Magdalen who suggested I consult with Mrs. Smyth, prompted perhaps by that poor woman's own losses. Mrs. Smyth, with her husband, ran a sewing machine and organ shop several blocks east of our own place, and Paddy had had occasion to consult them with regard to some of our own small machines. Mr. Smyth had a genius for mechanical work but he was known to drink too freely, the result, no doubt, of having lost six beautiful daughters in little over two years. He doted on the one remaining child, a little girl, and for her sake he continued to work a relatively normal day, but it was his wife who really ran the business. As well as sewing machines, they carried a few select items of haberdashery, although it was generally claimed that they made most of their money off sewing machine needles, an essential item which needed constant replacing.

I didn't know if it was possible to make a living selling such a tiny item as sewing machine needles, and had no wish to try doing so myself, but Mrs. Smyth had business connections with every bootmaker, tanner and leather worker in the city, and many outside of it, and I thank the good Lord that I had her to guide me through the negotiations needed to sell off Paddy's stock, place the apprentices in decent positions, and give up the lease on the premises. I believe that without her guidance, I might have fallen into the hands of a dishonest buyer and lost most of my money through sheer ignorance.

Aside from steering me toward men who could give me honest appraisals for the contents of the shop—men Mr. Smyth could vouch for through the Mechanics' Society— and then toward buyers for that stock, Mrs. Smyth encouraged me to begin immediately to plan for the long-term support and upkeep of my daughters. It was with considerable trepidation that I confessed to her my long-held dream of having a small farm, a place outside of town where I could hear myself think, where the stench of seal oil and fish did not permeate the air. Imagine my surprise, then, when she told me she thought it was a sensible and achievable goal.

Looking back, I suppose it was my mother who was responsible for my rather pessimistic attitude towards farming in the colony. Mother, having been raised in a milder climate, constantly lamented what could not be grown in the thin soil of the hills surrounding Petty Harbour. Never having had the experience of tree-ripened pears or oranges grown under glass, I never missed them, yet I had without knowing it, become convinced that a garden, worked in conjunction with fishing rooms, was the most we could ever manage on the island. Experience had taught me that the weather was never so bad that potatoes and cabbages did not grow to at least a moderate size, and the cows we owned had never starved even in winter, yet I did not take this knowledge and apply it more broadly until I discussed my hopes and plans with Mrs. Smyth.

In looking for a property suitable for farming, I turned naturally toward Kilbride and the Goulds, those two places having been settled by Petty Harbour families who could not find space to expand their family holdings in the contained area of the Harbour. Paddy had several cousins in Kilbride, and I had my own connections in the Goulds, for it had been the pattern for several generations for fishing families to move back into these areas and establish winter homes and summer gardens which they temporarily abandoned for the coast during the fishing season. As the market for fresh meat, vegetables and butter grew in St. John's, some of these people gave up the fishery and relied only on sealing for quick infusions of cash. Several times I left the children with neighbours and walked out to look at properties in Kilbride, but either the land was uncleared and unsuitable for cattle, or the price too steep for my limited resources.

I was in the last stages of selling off the stock in the shop, and had only three weeks to find alternate accommodation before the new tenant took possession of the premises, when I received a note from Mrs. Smyth asking me to step along for a word as soon as it was convenient. This was when she first told me that her husband had long owned property in the area later called Western Junction, and that he had heard of a small farm being offered for sale there. She had hesitated to bring it to my attention, there being no school and no relatives in the vicinity, and there being no real village, just a handful of farming families strung out along the road to Topsail. Mr. Smyth was traveling out that way by carriage the following day, and was willing to take me along for a look if I wished.

I did indeed wish, and it was everything I could wish for. It took many years before I could look at the property Mr. Smyth indicated as for sale without feeling the tug at my heart that I felt that first day. Compared to the large piece of land owned by the Smyths, or for that matter the land grants held by most of my neighbours, my own farm was small, and the meadows somewhat sloping, but compared to the garden in Petty Harbour it was Eden. It consisted of a small triangle of land, about seven acres, wedged between the path from Freshwater and the road to Topsail, with a one-storey, hip-roofed house, a number of outbuildings, several cleared meadows and a small patch of woods at the back. Across the main road, on the other side, the land dropped away to the Waterford River.

"The only way to begin a thing is to begin it immediately," I thought, and climbed down to walk over the area while Mr. Smyth conducted business with his tenant half a mile away. The house was empty and the fields had been neglected for a season, but the land had been worked carefully and the drainage looked good. Crossing the road, I climbed the short path down to the river. An osprey flew along the bank, between the shrubs and trees on either side of the water, and for the first time in many months I heard birdsong. Crouched by the side of the river, I could see water weeds and sticklebacks, and after my eyes adjusted to the sudden gloom of the foliage I could distinguish brown trout, waiting motionless in the stream for lunch to offer itself.

In later years, I came to know the river quite well, and caught there not just brown trout but brook trout and occasionally salmon as well as eels. Up towards Neville's Pond there were muskrat holes, and in the fall there were usually ducks of various sorts, but it was the sticklebacks that caught my imagination that day. The Waterford seemed such a small, safe river, a river where a child could play and not be drowned. I imagined Johanna and Min and Kate paddling in this cool, green paradise, catching sticklebacks and pulling flowers to braid into their hair, and I wanted that small farm more than I had ever wanted anything else in my life.

All those years in town had dulled my perception of the weather, and I was not really aware that this was a particularly dry year, and that the eight shillings a barrel that were being offered for potatoes was a relatively high price because of scarcity. The Waterford was normally a bigger river than it seemed, but by the time I realized that, most of my fears for the children had subsided to a relatively normal level. By the time we were driving back to town, I had made up my mind. I did not speak of my decision with Mr. Smyth, partly because I was somewhat shy of the man but also because I wished to let his wife do the negotiating for me. I had learned the hard way that a man might say anything in his cups, and I was afraid that if the owner knew how determined I was to buy the place it would suddenly be priced out of my reach.

I did not even look for another property while Mrs. Smyth and the lawyer who was looking after Paddy's will made the arrangements for me to buy Byrne's farm. I have to smile when I think of that name—I was determined that it would be Mrs. Aylward's Farm within the year, and yet it never was, though seven years later when I married again it was immediately referred to by all and sundry as Donovan's Farm. It's a good thing a woman is not raised to have too great an attachment to her name. As far as Mr. Donovan was concerned, it was my farm, but as far as the rest of the world went, it was his and that suited me well enough. Perhaps if he had had children, he might have wanted it for them, but that was something that he put behind him when he married me.

Those were the longest three weeks of my life. I kept packing up the household, selling everything I felt would be of little or no use in the country, and tried not to think what I would do if the sale fell through. I said little about it to the children, which I believe now was a mistake. One morning, a woman came to look at the kitchen dresser and she asked the price of Paddy's concertina, which I had stowed away in the lower shelves and forgotten about. I was about to let her have it for nothing when Johanna came in from school and burst into tears at the sight of it. I realized then that I had been so relieved to have my own life back again that I had forgotten that my girls had lost their father and were about to lose the only home they had ever known. I took the concertina back and stowed it in one of the barrels I was packing dishes in, and gave the disappointed woman the dresser at a bargain price.

After that I spoke a little to the children about the farm I hoped we would be getting, but they had never been on a farm and didn't really know what one was. When the papers were finally signed, I engaged a man with a cart and prepared to take them with some of our belongings out to Western Junction to see their new home. I had hoped Judith might come along, but she had made herself surprisingly scarce since Paddy's death, and I was unable to locate her in time. The girls were excited on the way out, but when we got there, they sat in the cart and looked around in puzzlement.

"Mama, where is the sea?" Johanna asked, and Min and Kate craned their necks around as if searching for their lost father.

"The sea is where it always is," I answered, pointing across country towards Petty Harbour.

"But why can't we see it?" I could hear something like panic in Johanna's voice. It was as if the sun were suddenly absent from the sky, or the grass had disappeared from beneath her feet.

"Come and see the river," I said to them, and began by lifting Kate out of the cart. "There are sticklebacks in it, and trout." The two older girls reluctantly jumped down and followed us across the road and down the bank to the river.

When I first came to Western Junction, it was like going to a place I'd known all my life, though I'd never been there before. It never occurred to me that my children wouldn't feel the same way. They hated the farm, they were afraid of the cows, the silence at night worried them, and they claimed that the noise of the crows and other birds at dawn gave them a headache in the morning. Min said the air was tasteless, and she longed for the stink of the harbour and the bite of soot on her tongue. In time, they became resigned to life in the country, and after the railway came and we opened the hotel they even began to enjoy it, but Kate was the only one who ever learned to love it.

That first day we did not stay over, but just unpacked the cart and went back to town, to sleep on a pile of mats and blankets on the floor of the almost empty shop. The stove was gone, so it was a sorry supper we made of it, but Mrs. Smyth walked down with her little girl and invited us to come and have breakfast with them the next morning. Little Anna had brought each of the girls a tiny sewing box, put out by the Singer Company as an advertisement for their machines, and my poor bereaved children hugged these to their chests and cried themselves to sleep.

As for me, I dreamed all night of potatoes at eight shillings a barrel and foolishly convinced myself that life at Western Junction would be like Petty Harbour without the fish and without the sea. I did not stop to think how lonely it would be for a woman with three small children. I only knew that I would not have to put up with Paddy, or even Paddy's cousins. The fact that the sea, which had been central to my life and the lives of my children, was now at least ten miles away in almost any direction, was a blessing that I had not had the imagination to hope for, nor did I have the sense to realize that you can miss something that you hate. There were times, in the years to come, that I missed Paddy and I missed the sea, but I never admitted it to anyone, least of all the children, and in time the longing went away forever.

August 4

Fine day but air is heavy. War declared. Dermot will be exempt because of his turned eye, and Min's little fellow is too small. Thank God we run to girls in this family.

The train made an unscheduled stop today. It left a package that Mr. Reid sent out from Johanna, a beautiful pink and blue blanket, woven from such soft, light stuff it is hard to believe it can be so warm. Kate says it is goat hair, but no goat I ever owned had wool like this. Kate has taken the heavy feather quilt off and replaced it with this beautiful blanket, though I think it is much too good to use. I confess, it is a relief for the quilt pressed down on me and made my already heavy limbs feel even more leaden, but I am so chilled, even with the sun streaming in, that I need a good warm cover. I cannot imagine where Johanna found such wonderful stuff.

There are movers and stayers in this world, and she was always a mover. When we went trouting, Johanna was willing to stop in one place for no more than ten or fifteen minutes before going on, up or downstream, to a better spot. Kate was a stayer, like me, rooted to the carefully chosen rill, convinced that eventual success was inevitable if one was stoical enough. Min was sometimes one, then the other. She often trailed after Johanna, but not without long, lingering looks back over her shoulder, at other times biding with us while sighing in the direction Johanna had taken.

We all got the same number of trout in the long run, I believe. To each his own, Mr. Donovan used to say. Johanna wanted a proper pole, but Min was satisfied with any stick, as long as it had a line, a hook and a bit of blackened cork. And a worm. Mr. Reid has shown me the remarkable flies he uses, and they are very pretty, but any trout would prefer a worm, I think. I certainly would if I were a trout.

Johanna has to be on the move. She was very patient for the first few years we lived here, and helped me as much as any grown woman could, but I could see it wasn't enough for her. When the note came from Mrs. Sands, with another attached from Mother Fowler, asking if I would be willing to let Johanna go to a family in town who needed a nursemaid, I suspected she had instigated the request herself, but what odds if she did. She was never argumentative or defiant, always a good daughter even if she did twist and maneuver to get her own way.

I hated to see her go to town, into service, but as she and Mrs. Sands told me, it wasn't as if she was a regular maid, more a nursemaid and companion for the children, and Mrs. Pedersen treated her like one of her own. She came home every second week for two days, and always brought some small thing for the other girls, and often something good to eat for me. I was always interested in food, and seeing that Johanna was with a Danish family, I often questioned her about the meals for I was sure they had to be quite different than those we had at home, but it turned out that Mrs. Pedersen was really Irish, only her husband was Danish.

In the fall, Johanna brought me sugar and a box of glass crocks so I could make up jams and jellies for the Pedersens. They sent them in a cart, and had to have the full crocks collected later when the snow was down, which seemed a lot of trouble. "It's only jam, after all," I said to Johanna, but she assured me that it wasn't only jam. It was jam with enough sugar, and no stems or twigs, and the crocks were clean and sealed with wax so they didn't go moldy.

"I'm learning a great deal more than you might think, Mama," she told me, and I've no doubt she was. She imitated Mrs. Pedersen in dress as well as she could, and she no longer made fun of my fussy ways in the kitchen. Instead, she quizzed me on every manner of household practice, and I have to say that some of her questions went unanswered because I simply did things the way my mother had taught me, without ever wondering why.

She once brought me a menu—I still have it somewhere—of a dinner party the Pedersens gave for a visiting merchant, and it wasn't so very unusual in nature as it was in variety and quantity. They served not just boiled mutton, but grouse pie, smoked Bath chop and roasted fowl, while any one would have done for a normal meal. Pudding was figged duff, gooseberry tart with clotted cream, and tipsy parson, followed by apples and Stilton. What apples—Sops of Wine and Pomme Gris from Quebec. I'm sure the names alone made the apples taste better. Oh, and Palestine soup. She brought me some of the roots in the spring, and I was able to grow the Jerusalem artichokes for myself.

It was that soup that got me started in the hotel business some years later. Mr. Donovan put his head into the kitchen door one morning and said that three gentlemen from the railway were out inspecting the line, and could I give them some dinner as they were famished. I told him I couldn't get any meat ready in time to give it to visitors and he laughed and said they told him soup and bread would do, for they were fainting with hunger. So soup and bread it was, though I had to pound the roots with a caulking mallet while they were still hot, which is not the best way. But with our own cream and three egg yolks and a grating of fresh nutmeg the Palestine soup was probably as good as Mrs. Pedersen's had been. I was fortunate enough to have a little cheddar cheese on hand, to make golden buck.

They drank the remains of the beer from the golden buck, and several more bottles as well, to wash down the soup and coddled eggs, and considering I had only half an hour to put it together I felt I had done pretty well by them. It was Mr. Reid, and two of the railway governors, and they were looking at the proposed new line. Mr. Reid stopped after, to try and pay for the meal, the foolish man, and asked me if I'd be interested in providing meals for people on the railway. He said it would be mostly summer work for special excursions, with only a few customers in the winter, and that he could provide me with a line of credit to lay in extra provisions. I told him he would have to discuss it with Mr. Donovan, at which he laughed and admitted they had already discussed it, and that it was Mr. Donovan who had suggested they try what they called my "decidedly excellent food."

I didn't know whether to laugh or cry. From the day I met Mr. Donovan, I had done nothing but criticize Ann Fitzpatrick's cooking, and when the railway went in I swore the whole lot of them would die of starvation if they continued eating at her house. In my mind, I planned menus and put additions on the house and once when Mr. Donovan stayed over at Sophie Maher's in Brigus Junction, I tormented him for days with questions about how the hotel was laid out.

That first time I went to St. John's with Mr. Donovan, so he could speak to Mrs. Smyth about wintering in the old tilt on back of their property, he asked me about doing some work in exchange for meals through the winter. He said if I would give him his dinner three days a week, he would cut all the wood I needed. I knew the men working on the road had been taking their meals at Mrs. Fitzpatrick's, and I asked why he didn't go there for his meals. He said he couldn't exist on a diet of burned potatoes and vinegar pie. The woman's house was tidy and moderately clean, but she must have damaged her tongue as an infant because she couldn't tell the difference between sweet milk and sour, and even with a fork she detected no difference between overcooked carrots and undercooked parsnips.

I tried my best to smother my smile, for there's no merit in delighting at someone else's failings, but he saw it and smiled back at me, and said "So it's settled, then. Monday, Wednesday and Friday at eleven," and before I could tell him no, that I didn't want men in the house, he had turned and was out the door. And then he was back again, fishing in his pocket, and handed me a small, flat bit of tin with a bent wire and an S stamped into it. "A present from Mr. Smyth. It's for threading needles," he added as he saw the puzzled look on my face. "In case the glasses aren't enough."

So all through the fall he came for his dinner, and I never had to say anything about the wood because it was always done, and so were a lot of other small chores that he needn't have bothered with, and he always said thank-you for the meal and made some appreciative comment about my cooking, which made me try a bit harder. I'd put a bit of ginger in the turnip, or add some vinegar and caraway to the buttered cabbage, or if it was nothing better than boiled rounders, I'd see that the potatoes were beaten with cream and a handful of dried chives, and I'd add extra raisins to the duff. The girls said nothing, though they seemed to like him well enough.

That Christmas, Johanna came home for the first week in January, and I don't know if it was her townie ways or if it was just her age, but she and Min decided to go jannying over to the Walshs', and they dug out a lot of Paddy's old clothes that I hadn't thought about in years. Paddy was a fairly small man, but Johanna was big like me and the clothes fit convincingly on her, especially when she took a hank of old horsehair from a worn cushion and fashioned herself a mustache and a scraggly beard which she fixed on with flour paste after she blackened her jaw. We did Min up in some old things of mine, worn finery that was not suitable in the country, and with a bit more of the horsehair stuffed down her blouse and a veil over her face, she looked at least ten years older than she was. At the last minute, Johanna uncovered Paddy's old concertina and brought it along to make a racket suitable to a mummer.

Off they went, down the road, and I thought no more about them since it was a green Christmas and the Walshs were no more than a mile away. There was rarely any trouble in a small community like ours with hardly a dozen families. I was working a new mat for Johanna's room in town, a pretty flower pattern with greens and pinks, and I settled down by the stove to wait until they got back.

It must have been close to midnight by the time I heard the door, and it wasn't just Min and Johanna, but Mr. Donovan too. Min had been crying and Johanna's disguise was gone and her face washed clean. Mr. Donovan hushed me as I tried to ask what had happened. "Let them go on to bed," he said, "I'll tell you all about it. You can ask them in the morning." He helped them out of their coats and things, which he piled on the settle, and shooed them out of the room before he pushed me back into my chair.

"Tell me right now," I said, "or I will . . ." I didn't finish because whatever I said I was going to do, I knew I would only cry.

"They're all right, I swear to God," he told me, and pulled one of the three-legged stools close to my knee. "I was over at the Walshs' when they arrived, and they fooled everybody for at least ten minutes. Min was gatching around like a grand lady, and Johanna played the concertina. There's no fiddlers around here with a concertina, so we were all baffled as to who they were. Then another crowd turned up, three fellows dressed in sailors' garb, black oil skins and sou'westers, but with nothing to disguise their faces but a bit of soot. They were looking for food, but more than that they were looking for drink."

"Oh, God help us and save us," I moaned. Mummering is

often used as an excuse to work off some grievance, and when liquor is involved, it often turns rough. It was also unusual for strangers to turn up in such an out-of-the way place.

"Hush," he said. "I'm telling it all. They aren't hurt." He stopped for a moment as if to sort out his thoughts. "Mr. Walsh was not inclined to be co-operative, not knowing who they were and all, and there was a different air about them than there had been to Min and Johanna, though we still hadn't identified them either. He gave them a glass of beer and some cake, and just ignored their suggestions that he break out the grog. I gave him a look to let him know that if he wanted them out, he could count on me. Then they began to dance, one of them playing Johanna's concertina, and one fellow, the skipper by my guess, grabbed Johanna and pulled her out onto the floor. It all seemed like a bit of fun, but I think he must have realized she was a girl, for in the press in the kitchen he made an attempt to get his hand into her clothes."

"Oh, sweet, gentle Joseph," I whispered, and put my head down in my apron.

"That's all it was, really, just fumbling at her jacket," said Mr. Donovan. "He was wearing trigger mitts and Johanna said that when she couldn't pry the one hand away from her buttons, she pulled the hand that was holding hers in the dancing up to her mouth and made to bite him. She said she didn't want to be unmasked, but she wanted to make him stop."

"I should think so," I whispered indignantly. "What on earth was the girl up to, trying to deal with such a thing herself. She should have screeched out for help right away."

"Well, no doubt you're right, but you know what young women are like. They think they can do everything for themselves." Then he gave me a funny look, and added, "Some older ones do, too."

"So what happened when she bit him?"

"Nothing, except his mitt came off in her teeth. He was

missing a thumb and she got nothing but a mouthful of home-spun. I suppose he figured if he did anything after that, it would be too easy to identify him so he made a signal to his friends and they left."

I felt then as if the world was falling away from my feet. All I could think of was the grasshook, and that disgusting man Thomas Salter.

"Now comes the hard part," said Mr. Donovan. "After the sailors left, the fun of being a stranger sort of disappeared and Min and Johanna unmasked. They had a bit of lunch and some hot tea, and then I offered to walk them home, seeing as there were strangers in the district. Min looked like she wanted the company, but Johanna was being a bit stubborn, so I let them go, thinking I'd walk behind them so I could keep them in sight. They were out the door and just going through the gate when Min let out the most unholy shriek."

I was afraid I was going to faint. "Go on," I said, "get it over with." Mr. Donovan leaned forward and patted my hand.

"It was the Walshs' dog, rigged up to fall out of the tree when the gate opened. It had been cut from stem to stern and the guts were hanging out. They hit Johanna right in the face."

By then I was crying and rocking, and trying not to make a noise as I didn't want the girls back in the kitchen seeing me like that. Mr. Donovan got up and made some tea to give me time to pull myself together.

"Are you really telling me everything?" I asked, choking on my own tears. "He didn't do more than try to get his hand into her clothes?"

"That's all it was, honestly. They seem to have taken their disappointment out on the dog." He pushed the tea into my hand, and lifted it to my mouth and made me drink a little. No man had made tea for me since the Bishop—I felt like a child. It had been seven years since Paddy died and in all that time I'd had no-one to lean on except Mrs. Smyth, who was kind enough but little more than a stranger, and the gentle way he urged the tea on me was my undoing. I told him all of it. I told him about Thomas Salter, I told him about my dog Egypt, I told him about Judith and about how Paddy died, I kept nothing back.

By the time I was finished, it was close to morning and I was exhausted—talked out and cried out. He moved all the things off the settle and eased me down onto it and covered me over with the coats the children had been wearing. By then the lamp had burned out and there was only a glow from the stove. I felt as empty and exhausted as if I had just given birth.

I didn't go to sleep for a long time, though, for once I was settled, Mr. Donovan did the most extraordinary thing. He picked up Paddy's concertina, undid the straps, and then he began to play it as quietly as a lullaby. Some of the tunes were strange to me, Portuguese or Spanish perhaps, and some were the old songs from home, but they were all so sad and so beautiful and I had never heard the concertina played like that, for Paddy had always made it jump and howl like a banshee. I fell in love with Mr. Donovan as he played the concertina, and if that isn't a miracle nothing is.

In the morning, when I woke, the kitchen was still warm and Mr. Donovan and Kate were sitting at the table eating fried potatoes and bread and butter. When he saw I was awake, he brought me some more tea.

"I'll be going to St. John's today, to report to the magistrate about the mummers. I'll give them the name you told me and the descriptions. I'm also sending a message to Manuels, to have the priest read the banns next Sunday," he said. "It's the only thing for it, now."

He was right, of course. There was no going back. We were married in the hungry month of March, and I counted the days. He made me teach him to sign his name, so that he wouldn't shame me in front of the children, but he never got beyond that in his lessons, though he taught me a thing or two.

Probably the only thing I didn't tell Mr. Donovan that night was that I wanted to have a railway hotel, but I didn't at the time know such a thing existed, though he probably did, having traveled in his early years. As the first stop on the railway, we never got many real travelers since on a good day it is only twenty minutes or so from St. John's, but being the first stop also made us the cheapest for picnics and society outings, and these were usually booked in advance so it worked out quite well right from the start.

Within a few years, I had my new house, and we used the old cottage for overflow and for the occasional long-term boarder, such as the station manager and the Big Galoot. Mr. Tooton made a postcard for us— a fine view showing both storeys and the verandah right off the dining room, with Kate in a carriage out front. We had six bedrooms, and a big back kitchen and pantries enough for a month of Sunday dinners. Even Sophie Maher didn't have as beautiful a prospect as the Waterford Valley affords. And she wasn't as good a cook as I was; Mr. Donovan said so.

August 10

Wet and still. Yesterday evening a pack of dogs came through the yard and two of the buggy harnesses broke when the horses bolted. One of the buggies was damaged and the horse is lame. Mumma would never allow Mr. Donovan to use poisoned bait or to shoot the dogs, but it is a trial. Mr. Walsh says that in the spring, someone posted a sign further along the road that said "For Sale—Delicious Lamb" and scribbled underneath was the comment "One thousand roving dogs can't be wrong."

Such a quiet morning—Monday is Sunday in the summer, as Mr. Donovan used to say. Kate thinks we should close on Mondays, but we get so few customers that it is very little trouble to stay open and it is good advertising to be open seven days a week. I can hear Dermot fixing the railing for the horses—it's past time he bestirred himself and did something useful. There was a day when I was as good with a hammer as I was with a mathook, but Kate's not like that—though I must admit she is much better with the accounts than I ever was, and I wasn't too bad.

During that first winter in Western Junction, I had to learn to fadge for myself. I was determined that the money left over from the sale of the contents of the shop would be used as sparingly as possible, in case things did not work out, but I had not realized how jarring this change in lifestyle would be for the girls. Like me, they had gone to school from an early age, but little else had been required of them except knitting and the care of their own clothes, and small chores such as cleaning lamps. The apprentices had filled the gully each morning, and I had emptied the slop buckets and night soil, so they had been exempt from even these regular duties.

I was determined that we should be self-sufficient as soon as possible, and had purchased two cows, as well as a pig and a number of fowl, to raise over the winter, and as part of my agreement with the Lees in Petty Harbour, who were still culti- vating my garden on shares, I obtained what I hoped would be sufficent fodder for the animals and vegetables for ourselves. Since I had to teach the girls their lessons myself, it was essen- tial that they help me with the household chores as there sim- ply weren't enough hours in the day to allow me to complete all that had to be done.

Each morning, I would rise and light the stove before going out to milk the cows and check my snares. It was an unusually good season for rabbits that year and I discovered that the woods at the back of my property were full of the creatures. I showed the girls how to push sticks into the ground to narrow the rabbit paths and lead them into the snares, but at first they absolutely refused to kill any of the rabbits they caught alive, even the ones that had had their eyes pecked out by the crows, although they were happy enough to eat them after they had simmered for an hour or so in a pot full of carrots, turnip and potatoes. Rabbits were all the fresh meat we had that first year, except for a fowl for Christmas, and every one I skinned for the pot was one less to eat my cabbages the following summer.

It was lonely for all of us in the beginning, but worst I think for Johanna who missed her classmates and the bits of music and such that she got from the nuns. She did what she could with her sisters, putting on a Tom Thumb wedding with Kate as the bride and Min as the groom, taking the part of the priest herself, but I was a poor audience, being usually too tired and too worried about the work left undone to enjoy it properly. After a time I got to know my nearest neighbours and arranged for two of the Walsh girls to come and learn their lessons with my girls. In exchange, their father took some of my butter and cream to town when he went to sell his own produce. Like my parents, I found myself writing letters and such for the people in the area who had little or no schooling, and like them I found that there were a surprising number of willing hands when there was heavy work to do that I could not manage by myself.

There were times when I longed for the companionship of a friend such as Judith, someone I could talk to without restriction, but the women I encountered were just as tired and just as busy as me, and there was a constraint between us because of my widowed status. The married men dared not speak one unnecessary word to me, and would not cross over the doorstep for fear someone would see and report them to their wives. Occasionally a boy from down Neville's Pond way would come round, ostensibly looking for odd jobs but in reality looking over Johanna, but lonely as she was Johanna quickly made it clear that she was not going to marry a farmer, and they would soon drift away.

Once the snow was down, things settled somewhat. The occasional trips to St. John's stopped, lessons became more interesting as I had more time to give to them, and the girls began to realize that their comfort was more or less in their own hands. I began insisting that they take their turn milking the cows in the evening, and it sometimes took all three of them as much as two hours, but the cows got milked and it was one less chore for me. Johanna was in charge of the cows, while Min looked after the pig, which was fed mostly on skimmed milk and dried caplin. Kate took a particular interest in the hens, and on Easter morning she presented me with the first of our own eggs. I boiled it up and shared it between the girls, two spoon-fuls each, and it was as fine an egg as the Queen herself ever ate.

I thought about potatoes a lot in those days. Once, before Paddy died, there was an agricultural fair held in St. John's, the best ever put on in the colony, and we all went. Paddy was bored by it, but I saw there a display of about eight kinds of potatoes from the west coast of the island, all different colours and sizes, each with its own special quality, and I marvelled at the variety. I had grown Black Minions in Petty Harbour, although I knew there were varieties that gave a higher yield. Father liked their dark red skins and their yellow interior flesh, and I liked them because they were such good eating, but I had always wanted to try others as well. Before I left St. John's, I had gone around all the small shops, looking for different varieties, and I now had four kinds besides the Minions, packed away in sawdust waiting for spring.

These days, we have Jenny Linds and the Setawayos, Green Mountain's and Kerr's Pinks, but in those days there were not such well-known kinds and it was necessary to watch your own crops and your neighbours' very carefully to try and discern some pattern in the growth. Some kinds of potatoes seemed more resistent to canker than others, and my own experience had been that the use of seaweed along with the caplin cut down on infection. We all used bottle kelp on cabbage—the substance in the knobs worked wonders with the white mag-gots—but the area around Petty Harbour was generally not suitable to the seaweed harvest and I was determined to find a potato that carried its own resistant properties.

In March, while the ground was still frozen, I bundled up the girls and we went with our neighbours to dig peat. Each farm then had a shallow pit dug into the ground for making fer-tilizer. We cut the peat with a sharpened shovel and then broke it into powder before spreading it in the pit. On top of the peat went gurry and guts, caplin and sewerage, anything and everything that could add a little richness to our poor soil. Every time a cart went into town with butter or vegetables or wood for sale, it came back with a load of rotting, stinking refuse that was added to the mix.

That day, as we walked home in the dark behind the cutter, I could have been as content as I had ever hoped to be, if it had not been for the children. I had dressed them in their oldest clothes, layer upon layer, but their hands were chafed raw by the shovels and their cheeks were burned red with the wind and cold. Seeing them drag themselves, one foot after the other, along the frozen mud of the path, almost weeping from exhaustion, I wondered if they would ever adjust or if I had made the biggest mistake of their young lives in taking them away from the town and moving them to the country.

As I pulled my cuffs off, I realized that my wedding ring had worn through from contact with the shovel and was caught on the wool inside the mitt. The children were cold and shaking from fatigue, so I had no time to fuss, just bent the soft gold open and pulled my hand free, and dropped the ring into a broken cup I had laid on the mantlepiece to be mended.

I made them a meal of hot oatmeal before putting them to bed, and then went to see to the milking. Usually the cows soothed me, but this evening I could not settle into the usual rhythm and they sensed how disturbed I was. As I walked back from the barn, a little owl that had been hunting mice in a rock wall nearby flew out of the dark almost into my face before going off into the woods. Later, I sat by the stove and prepared to say my rosary. I had promised myself I would say the rosary every night for a year for the souls of Mrs. Smyth's children, the only thanks she would accept for all her kind help, and the thought of her six girls, buried in the cold gound, while mine lay sleeping in the next room, added to my melancholy.

Three of Mrs. Smyth's children died in one week, of the cholera, and the others died within two years of the rest. Some blamed the sailors who came from foreign ports, some said it was the fault of the Irish immigrants who drank and failed to keep the Sabbath. In my own mind, I was quite certain that Dr. Carson had been right when he blamed the dirt and filth of the town for the deaths of so many from cholera and other diseases. The narrow, cramped houses kept what little sun we got from reaching into the streets, and there were dogs and pigs, with all their filth, in half the houses and cellars of St. John's. The stench from the seal oil vats made breathing a torture in May and June, and there wasn't enough lime in the entire country to clean the gutters and alleys of the place.

As I sat there, holding my beads and looking at the mark on my finger where my wedding ring had once been, I searched my heart for solace. The owl began calling from the woods, and I thought of the potatoes I grew in Petty Harbour, of sitting on a three-legged stool weeding them out and holding my breath—when the horseflies hovered and buzzed and landed on my outstretched arms, feeling the good luck passing into me from their tiny pitchy-paws. I knew then that I could not bring myself or my children back into the chaos of St. John's. Sure of my decision, and calm once again, I made the sign of the cross and said the Memorare before I began my fifteen decades.

August 17

Rain. The Sons of St. Andrew booked Squires Station for their annual dinner this year. Good riddance to them——I still haven't managed to get the boot marks off the ceiling from last year. And they claim the Irish are savages.

The sound of the train is so soothing in the evenings. I never guessed when they first put the tracks through that I could feel that way about it. Mr. Reid used to say that before the railway came, travel meant coaxing a jaded nag over the bogs and barrens or tossing about in a fog in a stinking jack-boat, with as good a chance of drowning as of reaching your destination. I suppose a great many people agreed with him, which is why they turned out in such numbers for that first run. I know that for the fishermen, who had no work between September and Christmas, the work on the railbed was very welcome.

When the railway was first built, it cut right through the woods in back of my property and I resented it. I was paid, of course, but it wasn't the money I wanted, it was the land. That bit of woods was my refuge when I needed to get away from the children. I could cut a few sticks to mend a fence or put in the stove, I could snare a rabbit, or I'd just sit on a log and think about what I had to do around the place. Sometimes, in the early days, I'd go and cut a bit of brouse for the cows—young birch and dogwood—to save on hay. The girls used to picnic back there, and I knew they were safe. Then the railway came and the woods were full of strange men, cutting and hauling and tearing everything up.

It was in January that the first train came through, a special excursion train full of judges and clergy and members of Parliament all invited by Mr. Loomis and Mr. Blackman. We only heard about it because Mrs. Fitzpatrick asked if she could borrow some of my cups and plates to feed them all. I didn't send over my best but I did send what I could afford to lose. I should have sent a hammer over, too, so they could break the biscuits without breaking their teeth. I had no intention of going to see the train come in, but the girls were so excited and they had made flags to wave as the engine went by.

We climbed up the path through what was left of our woods and stood on the bank, and you could hear the whistle all down through the valley, shrieking and howling like a banshee. All I could think was that I wasn't going to get much milk out of our cows that evening, or any other evening if this was to be a regular occurrence. Then the engine, with a dozen banners flying, came into sight, hurling along at a tremendous speed towards us, and I grabbed Kate and Min by the hand and hauled them back out of the way, and shouted at Johanna to move out of its path.

"It has to stay on the tracks, Mama," she called over her shoulder and began waving her flags. It went off the tracks twice at Manuels in the following month, so she wasn't quite right. I suppose they were slowing down by the time they got to us, getting ready to stop over at the shed near Fitzpatricks', so I got a pretty good look at it all. There were hundreds of people crammed into the two carriages, and men in the engine packed like herrings in a barrel, all shouting and carrying on. I couldn't help it—when the children started running after the train, I went along with them, and that's when I saw the engineer with his jacket all burnt like the Bishop's vest. I recognized Sir

William Whiteway, and some of the Parliamentarians, from engravings I had seen. They looked smaller and more ordinary than I had expected. In no time, the whole of the district was swarming with ladies and gentlemen.

By the time I got home with Kate, for Johanna and Min had stayed behind to help with the teas, my own place was half overrun. You'd think those townies had never seen a common cow, the way they gawked at my six, and the ladies were clucking and looking in the windows of what they called my "quaint little cottage." "Just like a doll's house," one of them said. I was as polite and helpful as I knew how, but I didn't think I was going to like having a railway in my back yard if this is what it led to.

It was a fine, sunny day, not too cold, so most of the ladies and gentlemen were walking about by the river and on the road, and after a time I was able to get back to my work. Towards the latter part of the afternoon, Johanna turned up with a lady she introduced as Mrs. Sands, and said she had offered to show her about the place. I was not pleased, but didn't wish to embarrass the girl by being inhospitable, and as it turned out Mrs. Sands was a pleasant and intelligent woman, who asked sensible questions about the hens and geese and even gave me a recipe for tonic to feed to the goat, which had been out of sorts for weeks.

Johanna set the table while I showed Mrs. Sands around and I think she was favourably impressed by the tidy way we kept everything. I had a nice bakeapple tart set aside for supper, and we had fresh bread Johanna had made herself that morning, with our own butter and cream and jam. There was a dish of eggs, and beets dressed with vinegar and mustard seed, and a slice of smoked ham that I had prepared myself in the fall, for I was able to get into the root cellar without fear of the frost getting in, it being such a mild day. I was glad of that ham after, for that night the temperature dropped like a stone and I'm told the harbour froze from Chain Rock to Riverhead in just two hours. I didn't dare open the door to the root cellar for ten days straight.

Once I discovered that Mrs. Sands knew Mrs. Smyth, I was able to relax and enjoy the unexpected company. I hadn't realized just how unused I was to receiving guests, or how much Johanna missed having someone other than myself to talk to and learn from. Later, when Johanna received an invitation to visit the Sands family in town—enclosed with a letter from Mrs. Smyth—I was happy enough to let her go, although I think I knew it was the beginning of losing my daughter. Father used to say your children are only on loan, and that is particularly true of daughters.

When the train turned and headed back to town, I stood with the girls and waved good-bye, and I felt a little differently about it than I had at the start of the day. In amongst those hundreds of people sitting on the red velvet carriage seats and standing in the aisles, was a familiar smiling face, not yet a friend perhaps but an acquaintance, that I had not had when the sun came up. Within the year, Johanna was gone to work for Mrs. Sands' friend Mrs. Pedersen, and I had married Mr. Donovan, and then Min got the school in Blackhead, even though she was only fourteen.

Nothing was ever quite the same again. It wasn't that I minded the changes, for some of them were changes for the better, but we had been happy when there was just me and my three girls. There were times, even years later, when I looked back with longing on those days when, snowed in or storm bound or even just on a rainy winter day, we stayed close to home and fire. We'd amuse ourselves with lessons and sewing or making some new concoction on the stove, and I might take the Bible down and read them one of the stories, Ruth or Jonah or Esther, one of the exciting ones, not one of the Begot chapters. All that came to an end.

In May of that year there was another excursion for the

members of Parliament, and this time I knew Mrs. Sands would be on the train, and Mrs. Smyth, too, as well as their husbands, and I laid on a tea that I would have been happy to serve to the Queen and Prince Albert. A month later there was the first official run to Topsail, with three closed carriages and an open one for the bands. The Walshes decorated their entire house with flags and banners, and I flew the Union Jack with the Native flag directly beneath it, although you could barely see them as our house was below the line then. The bands played "The Banks of Newfoundland" as they passed through the community, and Mrs. Fitzpatrick's heifer got on the track and had its leg broken, so we all had fresh meat for Sunday dinner later in the week.

I can't say I was really surprised when the riots started later that summer, although "riot" is too big a word for what amounted to a handful of sleeveens and sluts throwing rocks. I had heard all the rumors about toll gates and expropriation of land, and I was a bit nervous about it myself, but to think of Pinkie Mercer leading the charge, her hair flying loose and those big feet of hers flapping out from under her skirts, is shameful. Those men were only trying to make a day's wage the same as the rest of us. I thought to call it "The Battle of Foxtrap" was to give it a dignity it didn't deserve, but I liked the bit in the paper where they referred to Pinkie as an "ancient virago" and said she threatened to "let daylight into the stomachs of these invaders" with a fish fork. Well, the invaders won in the long run, and the railway wasn't so bad for Pinkie or anyone else on the route.

There were some unexpected benefits from the railway, too. Where the track was put down, the trees had been cut and burnt, and when the cuts grew over with young birch and alder, it was ideal for rabbits once more. I got some hemp sail twine and set my snares again, for I discovered that Mr. Donovan loved a rabbit pie every bit as much as I did. When he'd see me making the paste, and the pile of vegetables on the table, he'd always say "The wind did blow and the leaves did wag, along came Keziah and put me in her bag." This was just to tease me a little, for the real words were "along came a little girl," and I was neither little nor a girl, though when he teased me I felt as if I were both.

The railway made it easier losing the girls, as well, for they could come and go more often. After a few years, Robert Walsh gave an acre of land to Bishop Mullock for a school, and Min was given the post so we had her back at home for a time before she married. They called the school St. Ann's. Some said it was named for Ann Fitzpatrick, because the men who used to go to her place for cards and a meal didn't want their wives to know where they were and used to say they were going to St. Ann's for a meeting. If that's true, I'm sure the Bishop didn't know that when he named it.

After the Fort William station burned down in town and they built the new station, they decided to move the track down from the ridge into the valley. Then Mr. Reid and the governors had what Mr. Donovan called the Palestine Soup Summit and they decided to put the new station on O'Flanigan's land, on the other side of the river just opposite us. They built that small bridge, so passengers could get to the road, and not coincidentally to our new hotel.

Poor Kate. The bridge went right over her favourite trouting spot and the footings destroyed the pool. While Johanna always used a rod and Min and I relied on poles, Kate had a talent for hand-catching trout, and she insisted they tasted better because they hadn't been hooked or damaged in any way. She would sit on the bank in the spring and spot the quick flash as the trout moved under a rock and then, with her petticoats dragging in the water, she would stretch her arm up under the rock until she felt the slippery prey in the farthest corner and, almost without fail, she'd have it caught behind the head and flung up onto the bank in a second. Min tried it once and got an eel by mistake and you could hear the shrieks all the way up to Neville's Pond.

But of course the biggest change the railway brought was Mr. Donovan. I can hardly remember how I managed without him. It wasn't just the work, though the Lord knows that it was wonderful to have a man around for the heavy hauling, especially one who was so quick and clever with his hands as Mr. Donovan. It was more that I had someone I could be weak in front of. He teased me a lot, but not about the things that really hurt, and I never knew him to say an unkind word about me or anyone else. Just as Kate had a gift for catching trout and Johanna had a gift for putting a flower in a glass or pinning a brooch on a dress so that it was perfectly placed, Mr. Donovan had a gift for forgiveness. He saw all the weaknesses in my too-human heart and he forgave every one of them.

August 18th, 1914

Dear Aunt Johanna,

Auntie Kate has gone to town for supplies and I am looking after Nanny, but she has been asleep all afternoon and I can't find the book I was reading. I think Dermot put it in the stove as I found what looked like the boards when I went to make tea for a customer. Poor Aunt Kate has enough to worry about so I didn't tell her, and besides I think perhaps I deserved to lose it as I was so absorbed in reading that I forgot to check on the cows and the new one got out onto the track. Dermot found her just in time so at least we won't be eating salt beef all winter. He didn't tell on me about the cow, so I won't tell about the book.

Nancy Walsh calls Dermot 'Blue Eyes' (one blew east and one blew west), which is rather mean as he can't help being born wall-eyed, but it does make me laugh when I think of it. As you may have guessed, we are still fighting but I have rather gotten over my intense dislike of him, which is just as well as I think we are all going to see even more of him in the future. The very last thing Nan said to me before she became ill was that I was to stop teasing Kate about him, and now that I've stopped I realize how much it hurt her. I wish I would hurry and grow out of being thoughtless half as fast as I am growing out of my shoes.

Mama told me that I might be able to go to you next summer, and oh, how dearly I would love that. I really can be quite useful around a hotel—just not one that has cows—and I can't bear the idea of coming here when Nan is gone. I think Aunt Kate will be making new domestic arrangements before long, and Mama is so absorbed in the shop and with Jimmy that she hardly notices me these days.

I wish I had something cheerful to say to you, but it all

seems to be bad news these days. Nan is so thin now you would hardly recognize her. The talk in town is of nothing but recruiting for the new regiment (Mrs. Miller says I might as well go to the Boston States, as when I grow up there will be nobody left here for me to marry because they will all have been killed by the Huns, which is not very flattering to our soldiers). There is bread pudding for afters, my least-favourite. But you-know-who likes it so we must all suffer.

The blueberries are very good this year so Mama will be sending you a case of jam, which I guess is cheerful news, but that's about the only nice thing I can think of so perhaps I had better end here.

Please don't worry about Nanny. She doesn't seem unhappy. She just sleeps or talks to herself all the time, though it is such a mumble I can hardly ever make out the words. Auntie Kate tends to her as if she were a newborn baby, so gentle and kind. Now I've made myself cry, and I've probably made you cry as well. So much for trying to end on a cheerful note.

Mama says to write and tell me what I will need to bring when I come to Boston so that I can begin the sewing this winter. I am longing to see you. It is so quiet and sad around here now, not like it was when Nanny was well.

Your loving niece,
Elizabeth

P.S. The girl has quit again, and I shall have to tell Auntie Kate when she gets home.

P.P.S. Is it true that the Sacred Heart girls do all their lessons in white gloves? I shall need at least a hundred pairs as I find it impossible to keep them clean even when I'm doing nothing whatsoever.

August 18

*Lizzie spent the day here. Mumma dictated her recipe for
Black Currant Jelly which went something like this:*

> *"Put berries and a little water in skillet. Bring to
> boil and let simmer. You will know yourself when
> they should be taken off the stove. Strain and add
> sugar which has been previously warmed. You will
> judge for yourself how much sugar. Now bring
> strained juice and sugar to a boil and let boil for
> as long as you think right. Put in crocks and seal.
> This jelly should be clear and firm and of good
> flavour. It will keep for years."*

*L*izzie gave me a wash today, my hair too, and then she
combed and braided it back into its bun. When she
held the mirror for me to see, I got a shock. I look like that little monkey Judith had, all eyes and skull. Paddy hated that
monkey, more even than he hated Judith, I think. I always
thought there was a resemblance between them—Paddy and the
monkey—which might account for his aversion. They were
both so small and had such a thin, hairy pelt, and they were
never still, just jumping and twitching and jerking around all the
time, never still for a moment.

The first time Judith brought that monkey into the kitchen,
it gave me such a turn. She had it down in her bosom, and when

she drew back her shawl and there was the ugly little face peeping out with those big, cold eyes, I thought for a moment she had a baby there at the breast. Poor thing, neither chick nor child to love and then the best she could do was that ugly little monkey. There was a woman had a shop in the east end, on Wood Street, who had a monkey that her husband gave her when her baby died, and people used to say she really did put it to the breast. Judith wasn't that touched, or if she was she was cute enough to hide it. I couldn't imagine where she got such a thing, or where she got the money to buy it, for I'd been led to understand the nasty little beasts cost a pretty penny, and I was half afraid to ask. Not that Judith was ever a bad girl, but some of those women who worked on the wharves were so pressed to make a shilling to feed their families that they would sometimes accommodate a sailor out of desperation.

She told me she got the monkey from a man on a boat from St. Peter's. They were offloading the contraband, and had only one keg left when the customs man came by—not the one they had paid off but another, for the shifts had been changed without notice. This was a new fellow in a spanking new unifom. One of the men took the keg of brandy and dropped it down into an empty five kintal cask that was sitting by the wharf. The customs man was going up and down the wharf, poking his nose into all the boxes and barrels, and it was just a matter of time before he saw the keg, which was exposed in the bottom of the empty barrel. Judith went over to one of the splitting tables and came back with a bucket of half-rotten cod livers and poured the oil into the barrel, and all over the edge and outside as well.

It's a pity men aren't as particular about their ordinary clothes as they are about their uniforms, for it would save a great deal of work for their wives. That barrel was so big that there was no way the excise man could see down into it, or even tip it over, without getting a good hold on it and getting rancid oil all over his nice new government suit. Judith said you could tell by the way he was looking around him that he suspected, so she went and got another bucket of the foul stuff and slopped it over his boots as she passed him to pour it into the barrel. The keg must have been made by a very conscientious cooper, for the brandy survived not only the drop off the Frenchman's shoulder into the barrel, but it sat in that oil for two days before they could get it out without being caught and there wasn't a whiff of anything but the best Napoleon when they drained off the contents.

Paddy said Judith should have asked for the brandy instead of the monkey, but that's just because the poor creature bit him when he tried to make it do tricks. Judith had to have some comfort in her life. She used to say "I kill myself on the wharves and when we clew up, I know I won't have a copper to put on my eyes," and it was true, too. When the poor monkey got sick, she went to Dr. Cuddihy because he was the only doctor who would look at the creature, but he just poked it in the belly a few times and then took her money. She sat with it in the corner of my kitchen, near the stove, and coaxed it to drink the St. Jacob's Oil off a tiny spoon I had from Mother, and when it died, even Paddy was careful not to make fun of her grief.

It wasn't long after that I was coaxing Paddy with the spoon myself. I told Judith he'd probably got a dose from some girl down behind the courthouse, but given the way Paddy ate and drank and lived, it's as likely he just suffered from a bad gut. After the shop closed in the evening, he'd take tobacco and rum and a plate full of doughboys and eat them standing at the table. Then it was off to the races on Flower Hill, or dancing on the tables and playing the concertina in some hell-hole grog shop until all hours of the morning. It would give anyone the cramp.

It started off easily enough, with a bit of griping and complaining and Paddy off his feed for a week or so, but then it got worse at night and off he went to Dr. Cuddihy for a cure. Inflammation of the bowels, Cuddihy told him, and wrote up a recipe for Mr. McMurdo. I don't know how much of the medicine Dr. Cuddihy told Paddy to take, but he was never a man for short measure, so I expect it was a good dollop. Paddy wasn't one to hold back, either, and he seemed set to make a thorough job of his own destruction. He was swilling the stuff back at a great rate, and sending Johanna or one of the apprentices down to the pharmacy every day or so for another bottle, until Mr. McMurdo refused to sell him any more. By this time, Paddy had the colleywobbles and was on the chamber pot half the night, and his hands were shaking so badly he could hardly hold an awl.

I thought he was wasting his time taking that old stuff Cuddihy suggested, but he was so miserable, even snapping at the children, and the black dog was so well settled onto him that I was ready to do anything he wanted just to stop his griping. It was Judith who reminded me that McMurdo wasn't the only chemist in town, and she offered to go into the Cross and get what I needed there. Paddy's tongue and mouth were so swollen by then he could hardly speak, and the spit was running out of his mouth and down his chin like a baby. He could barely sit up, never mind stand, so I had Judith get the medicine for him, but it just made him vomit. After that I sent for Dr. Cuddihy again, but it was no good for the doctor was on a randy and didn't sober up for another two days.

I'll never forget the look on Cuddihy's face when he found out how much of his medicine Paddy had managed to choke down. By this time Paddy had been half unconscious for four days, and it was less than a week more before he died. "Kidney failure" was what Cuddihy put on the death certificate, but Mr. McMurdo told Judith and half the town that it was mercury poisoning and that Cuddihy should have been prosecuted.

I got the priest in to Paddy before he went, but I doubt he could have made much of a confession as he hardly knew what was what, but at least he got the last rites, and I made sure he got a proper funeral, with all the societies in their uniforms and capes and sashes and the Fort William Volunteer Fire Department all done up in red and green and their banner draped over the coffin. I sat home with the girls, and Mrs. Smyth and Judith and some of the other women came to be with me, and afterwards the men came from the graveyard and stopped on their way to the tavern and offered their condolences. Mr. Smyth was very kind and said he would be happy to help me with selling the machines in the shop, and Mr. McMurdo brought a bag full of barley sugar for the children. Dr. Cuddihy was at the church, I was told, but he didn't stop to see me after and he didn't go to the tavern but bought a bottle and went straight back to his surgery, they said. I never laid eyes on the man again in my life.

I didn't see too much of Judith either, after Paddy died. It seemed as if she was avoiding me, and it troubled me a good deal. I saw her going through the back way one morning when I was packing up, and called her in to have a cup of tea. She stopped, but with reluctance.

"I can't visit, Keziah," she said. "I've got a hobble, one you'd rather not know about, and it can't wait." By that I understood she was helping to take contraband off one of the ships in the harbour.

"Judith, the excise men are going to force you off the wharves if they catch you again, they're just looking for an excuse." She'd been into it with the customs office more than once.

"Let them try," she said with a laugh, just like her old self. "God's vengeance on the lot of them. May the dogs lap their blood when they die, and the ground sink beneath their graves."

The Irish take their curses very seriously, so I clicked my tongue at her.

"Don't go ill-wishing them, Judith, they're only doing their jobs. And you won't get away with it forever."

"You're the one to be talking. There's some think they can get away with murder around here." She flung the words at me and turned on her heel and was gone.

It worried me, Judith misunderstanding me that way, just when I needed her friendship more than ever. I was only thinking of what was best for her. She wasn't smuggling for the money, I'm certain of that—she just had a scunner against every tidewaiter that ever drew breath on this earth.

"Married in black, you'll wish yourself back," was the old rhyme. I had been married in black, after the Bishop's funeral, and here I was in black again, with three fatherless children to care for. I can't say I didn't worry, but after all the long days of Paddy's illness, and the bad temper and moodiness, and even worse the pathetic look of him trying to hold a spoon or climb the stairs, it was a relief to have it over. Poor Paddy, in his good days he used to go into the fish sheds on the harbour and he'd hook a half-kintal weight onto his little finger and then he'd take a pencil, and with the same hand he'd write "Talamh an 'Eisc" on the beams over his head. He said that meant "The Land of The Fish" in Irish, and it was what they called Newfoundland where he came from. By the end he couldn't lift the pencil alone.

It took just six weeks for Paddy to die, the longest weeks I've ever suffered through, longer even than these weeks I'm living now. The shop was going to wrack and ruin, with the apprentices saucing the customers and the journeymen just waiting to steal the place out from under me, and finally I could just shut the doors on it and get ready to sell up.

It might have been true, what I told Judith. Maybe Paddy did catch the clap from a trollop. The girls always liked Paddy.

Once I was down at Ayre's, looking at a bit of lace for Johanna, and Paddy went by on the sidewalk, bouncing on his heels the way he always did and looking like a golden angel in the sun, with a joke or a compliment for every woman he passed. The girl in the shop stopped and looked out the window at him, and this small sigh escaped her. "Now, he's the lovely fellow, isn't he," she said to me. So I just thanked her, and that's when she realized that he was my husband and she blushed and dropped the scissors. When I got home I found she'd cut me an extra yard of lace by mistake, but I didn't bring it back for fear of getting her into trouble.

August 30, 1914

Dear Johanna,

Min was out yesterday to see Mumma and to celebrate little Jim's birthday, and she suggested I write to you, for I have been very worried about the business lately. Even before she became so ill, we had all three discussed the necessity for making some changes, for Mumma was finding it difficult to keep up her end of things. She is now eighty-four and everyone agrees that until this stroke she was a wonder, but since she broke her hip she has been finding the volume of work to be almost too much, and I don't hesitate for a moment to admit that I have never had her stamina.

We had talked over the possibility of moving into the small house again, and leaving the hotel to a manager. Mr. Samuel Neal of Manuels, who is married to one of the Walsh girls, has been enquiring about buying the hotel, but of course it is not for sale. He might, however, consider taking on the management, and with me next door to keep an eye on things and do the accounts I think we could maintain control. To be blunt, I have never been good at anything but the dairy and I would very much like to get back to my cows. At the moment, Dermot is caring for them and he is very good about it but he is a little heavy handed and knows it. It is not a comfortable situation for us or for the cows.

As you are in the business yourself you will understand when I tell you that things are not as they once were. When Mumma took on the station, she had only to look after the railway men and occasional travellers. The Society dinners and picnics that followed are an enormous amount of work but they are seasonal and we always had a chance to recover from them during the winter. Now, however, there is not just the railway but also passing trade and in the evenings we have almost as many automobiles as buggies in the yard. It is often midnight or later before we can close the doors. Mumma might have managed a roadhouse as she has the strength of personality, but I am neither capable nor willing to do so.

And while we are on the subject of Mumma, I have to tell you that I am very worried about her also. Father Roche has been coming by every few days, and Johanna I daren't say this to Min for she won't hear a word against any cleric, but I believe he is tormenting Mumma in her last days. He stays talking to her for an hour at a time and when he leaves she is agitated and restless. She has been rambling on about Papa for the last few days, in a very distressing way. At first I thought she meant Mr. Donovan, for she rarely spoke of Papa, but she didn't ever call Mr. Donovan 'Paddy' and it is Paddy that is on her mind.

I do not remember Papa at all, except that he was rather noisy and he laughed a good deal. I still have the mechanical chicken he gave me for my second birthday—I let Lizzie play with it and she broke the spring—and I recall that he would stand me on his boots and dance around the room, but sometimes I believe I don't really remember these things at all but only that you told me about them. Mumma said once that when we moved here, we left Papa's ghost back in the city. Well, I believe he has finally found his way to us, for the house feels full of her memories of him.

Dermot says Father Roche is out to damage Bishop Fleming's memory and that I should refuse to allow him to see Mumma again. I wish I could, but he is a very powerful man and if he were to decide to work against us, we would certainly lose all the Catholic Societies which are the backbone of the business.

If you are writing to Min, please do not mention my

feelings about Father Roche. I am glad you are having Lizzie next year, for Min is very taken up with little Jimmy and now that her stepbrothers are gone, it is rather lonely for the poor child. I know you have offered to pay her school fees but if things work out with Mr. Neal I hope to contribute something out of my share of the profits. If Lizzie is to go to school with well-to-do girls, she must not be ashamed of her clothes, and I have no doubt that she will take advantage of the education she is being offered. When she entered Grade One at school, she was the only child in the class who could successfully add fifteen shillings to six shillings to make one pound one shilling. She will be a credit to us all.

If anything of significance happens here, I will send a cable to let you know but we realize that you will not be able to get away. I cannot tell you how it helps to be able to write openly to you about what is on my mind. Min is a great support but rather rigid in her ways at times. I may need your help in another matter in the coming months, but I know I can count on you as Min will listen to you when she will not listen to "baby sister".

I was about to write that you will be in my prayers, but the truth is that I am so tired these days, I most often fall asleep without saying them. I remain, however, your loving and devoted sister,

Kate

August 30

Fine, blowy day. Kaiser William was on the track again and the engineer refused to stop, because of his name. Mr. Walsh says he will go to court over it. Mr. Reid offered to buy the carcass and sell it off to raise money for the new regiment. Mrs. Walsh has been in tears all day, says she wanted to change his name to Prince of Wales but wasn't sure how to go about it. Mumma worse. Doctor says it won't be long now.

I believe I have taken a turn for the worse, as the doctor was here. I thought it was just a dream, for I am so confused these days, but I can see the bottle of medicine on the table so I know he must have been here. I will not take it. I thought I could not move my limbs again, but when I finally made myself try to lift first my finger and then my hand, they both moved, but thinking about doing it wore me out and I have no wish to try again.

There is no cure but death for what is wrong with me, and medicine more often makes things worse, as it did for Paddy. I am quite ready to go, I think, though there was something I had on my mind to do that now escapes me. Everything is such a muddle in my head—my brain is moithered. Kate was reading me a letter from Johanna and I thought it was from the Bishop's sister who is dead and forgotten this long while. She was a dear little woman, not at all like my own Johanna but very capable nevertheless. How I laughed when she told me about the time the Bishop stopped in the middle of one of his sermons when she was coughing her way through the mass, and bawled out, "Johanna, go home out of it!"

Kate says she has sent for the parish priest, but for some reason it is Father Roche who is coming again instead. I cannot take to that man—he is too ambitious and too political, with none of dear Bishop Fleming's warmth or generosity. They say he is a sick man himself, almost as sick as Bishop Howley, and may not live to be consecrated. I don't know why the vicar-general would come all the way from St. John's to bring the sacraments to an old woman when the parish priest is available. I wish it was Father Walsh I was to make my last confession to, for there is something I have forgotten and I know Father Roche will try to hurry me along, for even when I know exactly what I want to say, I am hardly able to string two words together to speak them aloud.

I'm very glad Father Roche was not my confessor after I married Mr. Donovan, for I don't think he would have laughed as Father Walsh did when I told him my first great sin.

Before Mr. Donovan came to Western Junction, I had read in the papers about the relief portraits of the Bishop done by the Irishman Hogan, and made a special trip into town to see them. Mrs. Smyth was busy with the shop and couldn't come up over the hill with me, so I went to the Cathedral by myself, and went in, and there was one portrait of him blessing Bishop Scallan as he died, and in the other he has his hand on the head of a child. They were both very nice, but they did not make me sad which I had somehow hoped they would. Then I went up to the altar rail to say a prayer for the dear Bishop's soul, for his crypt is beneath, and under the altar was The Redeemer in Death, and oh, I could hardly breathe, it was so beautiful, and I wept at that poor white figure, like a man frozen in the snow, so young and perfect.

The first time I saw Mr. Donovan, my beautiful new husband, in his natural state, so pale and handsome with his strong, long limbs, I wept, just as I had in the Cathedral. I did not confess my pleasure to Father Walsh, for as a married woman I had a right to that, though after those dreadful years with Paddy I had long ceased to expect it or even long for it. But I thought that to kiss my dear husband's feet and think of Our Redeemer was wrong. My only difficulty was in determining exactly what kind of a sin I had committed, for it was not exactly against the Second Commandment regarding the Lord's name, nor was it the third Deadly Sin of lust, nor was it obstinacy in transgression—the fifth sin against the Holy Ghost—and it was certainly none of the Sins Crying to Heaven for Vengeance. But a sin I was sure it was, and so I confessed it.

I do not know why Father Walsh should find it so funny that I thought my Mr. Donovan had the feet of the Dead Christ, but I was quite content that my penance was to go home and love my "fortunate" husband 'til death should part us. Looking back now, I suppose it was not exactly the kind of sin he was used to hearing, nor perhaps the kind of remark the women of the parish might make about their husbands.

Oh, I didn't know where to look after I came out of the confessional and there were the three Norman girls with their mouths open, staring at me like sheep, and the fits of giggles still coming at intervals from behind the door of the priest's section. I have heard Mrs. Norman use her husband's name in conjunction with that of the Redeemer on many occasions and on none of them was she praising him. Still, I would not have cared to raise the matter with Father Roche, for he has such a rigid opinion on so many things, and if he were to smile it might crack his face as if it were already on a marble tablet next to Bishop Scallan and Bishop Fleming.

Ned Roche is here. He came into the room, with Kate creeping in after him, and looked down at me and asked "Are you making your soul?" "Yes," I said, "and are you making yours?" I did not mean to say it, but seeing that cold, arrogant face made it slip out. I do not know what came over me. I was right about him having no sense of humour. Kate tried not to laugh but I could see it was a struggle. Then he left me to examine my conscience and came back after supper.

I make light of Father Roche's visit, but I cannot catch my breath and I have a sense of dread that I have not felt in many years. He instructed me on the Devotions for Confessions and reminded me that as well as the Deadly Sins and Contrary Virtues, and the other personal transgressions against God and man, there are also nine ways of being accessory to another's sin. He gave me a meaningful look then, and Kate, who had come in at the door, turned white and pulled away as if she would hide behind the wallpaper if she could. Whatever he has on his mind, I do not know, but it is most disturbing.

There is something I have forgotten that is very important, something I meant to include in my confession. I am so confused. I believe it has something to do with Paddy, but I cannot recall what it was. I wish some other priest had come, so that I could ask to be helped with this, but Father Roche is not easy to speak to even for someone who has an obedient tongue. I have made my confession and been anointed, but it has brought me very little relief. My agitation grows every moment, and though Father Roche said I must excite in my breast heartfelt sorrow for all sins, even those I have forgotten, I do not believe that I can be assured of redemption unless I can name the sin. It is on the tip of my tongue, but I cannot quite form the words.

September 2

*Cold, wet day. Mumma was quite strong last evening when
Father Roche annointed her—she told him clearly in front
of Father Walsh that Bishop Fleming was no saint, but was
better than a saint for he was just an extraordinarily good
man—but she is slipping away today. She murmurs constantly about Papa.*

Where have I put the shroud? I won't be waked in one
of those nasty brown robes. I have had my plain
linen shroud ready since Mr. Donovan died, washed and
starched and ironed once a year since on the day of his death.
I'm sure I must have told Kate where it is—in the bottom of
the old Labrador box with that tin chicken she wore the paint
off, and Johanna's christening dress, and my few precious bits
and pieces. Did I give Mr. Conroy the deed to the farm?

But I must remind Kate about the shroud. I have the most
horrible feeling, thinking about that—being laid for everyone
to look at, like the Irish do. She will draw it over my face, I am
sure.

I laid Paddy out in the shop, for I didn't want him upstairs
with all those men traipsing in and out, and there was no space
below except the kitchen. How did I get him down there? It's
such a blur. It wasn't the apprentices that helped me, for they
were all out getting drunk. I believe it must have been Judith.

"The only difference between a wake and a wedding is that there's one less drunk at a wake," she said.

What a wake it was. I put a big stone on top of the salt meat to firm it up, and cooked up a huge pot of potatoes and cabbage and carrots from the garden in Petty Harbour. A group of the firefighters volunteered to sit up with him through the night so I could tend to the children, and it was worth the price of the tobacco and pipes to get a few hours sleep. One of the men fell asleep and they painted his face with green boot polish and he didn't discover it 'til he got home and his wife gave a shriek at the sight of him, thought he'd caught the plague or something. Lord, what a racket they made. Paddy loved a good, rowdy wake. "There's no fun around here," he'd say. "Nobody's dying!" Well, they had a bit of fun that night, though I think the only jig Paddy danced was when Judith was helping me take him down over the stairs.

Yes, it must have been Judith. She was as strong as a man from working on the docks, and she brought in her old hand-barrow to move him. We came down over the stairs, making the narrow turn, and the stiffness hadn't set in for his legs were dangling down at the knees, tapping out a jig on the steps like a dancing doll, and his head lolled back and forth in a most comical way. We set some boards over two puncheon tubs Judith hauled in from the road, and I stripped him down. He hadn't been shaved in weeks and I had a hard job taking the gingery whiskers off his cheeks without marking his face up.

Poor Judith. I remember now, Mr. Donovan made inquiries after we were married, and said she'd been found face down in the harbour. She was into something a lot bigger than she guessed, I suppose.

What was it Judith said about Paddy? Was it something rude about his manhood? I know I was shocked. I was pouring the water down over him, giving him a good scrub—he was in need of one, had the smell of rancid butter in his hair always—

and Judith remarked on the fine condition of his privates. Oh, I was so taken aback, looked her right in the eye and then, something dreadful . . . I don't like to think about this. Judith said she didn't blame me, but she gave me such a look, half sorrowful and half frightened.

God Almighty, I think I understand now, it was the mercury. Judith had asked me when she went to get the mercury if I needed the Rush's Pills or something for treating the Louis Veneri, and I said I'd seen the sores, that he needed it for the clap. It wasn't exactly a lie, he might have had it, I just said it because I was angry at him. Judith got enough medicine for the two of us, for me and Paddy, but I didn't take it because I hadn't been with him since I hit Kate with the hat. When she saw him—saw his body—he was as clean as a newborn baby. She wouldn't look me in the eye after that—stayed with me through the wake, then more or less disappeared.

I shall never forgive myself for that, for hitting the poor little baby, and her blue with cold. I am glad Ned Roche reminded me, for I confessed it once, but the priest didn't listen, called me a foolish, trivial woman. I wish the Bishop was here, that I could confess to him, for then I could die with a clean conscience. My longing to confess is so great, and his longing to forgive was always written on his face, so that I feel I have only to say the words and . . .

September 4

Mumma died this afternoon. As she struggled to sit up, Dermot came forward to help me, and when he lifted her in his arms, she said a most piteous voice "I should never have hit Kate with that hat." He stroked her hair as if she were a child and said "Don't worry, go to sleep." Then she gave him the most sweet, beautiful smile and a few moments later she was gone. We will have the banns read after the funeral—we have waited long enough.

Sept. 6, 1914

Monsignor Emmet Murphy
All Hallows, Dublin

My Dear Emmet,
    Thank you for your letter of August 26th. It arrived in record time and was waiting for me when I got back to St. John's last night. You might wonder at my being absent from town at such a critical time, given the news from Europe, but I am closer to the pulse of government when in Topsail than you might think. For many decades now, Topsail has been more of a summer resort than a fishing and farming community. I am invited to say grace frequently, with our own leading families, of course, but also with those of the separated brethren, and three nights ago I even broke bread with a Hebrew shopkeeper who carved a boiled ham with surprising skill. One must extend one's influence whenever the occasion to do so arises. What might be frowned upon in town is tolerated, even encouraged, out here in the country where I have access to some of our most important politicians and merchants. Unlike at least one of my predecessors, when I "sup with the devil" I bring a very long spoon to table.
    Regarding my request that you search the record for any references to a Keziah Osborne, also called Mrs. Patrick Aylward and Mrs. Patrick Donovan, I am relieved to hear that your search has proved fruitless. One hears rumors and it is as well to proceed with caution. As her confessor it would have been my duty to raise the matter had I any real suspicion of impropriety. The female in question had suffered a paralytic stroke, which ultimately proved to be fatal. She was of little importance to anyone, but I thank you for your discretion in this matter.
    With great respect and many thanks for your kindness, I beg to subscribe myself.

                Your brother in Christ,
                Edward Patrick Roche
                Vicar General
                Archdiocese of St. John's